Midnight Unleashed

Also From Lara Adrian

The 100 Series
For 100 Days
For 100 Nights
For 100 Reasons
100 Series Digital Boxed Set

Midnight Breed Series
A Touch of Midnight (prequel novella FREE eBook)
Kiss of Midnight
Kiss of Crimson
Midnight Awakening
Midnight Rising
Veil of Midnight
Ashes of Midnight
Shades of Midnight
Taken by Midnight
Deeper Than Midnight
A Taste of Midnight (ebook novella)
Darker After Midnight
The Midnight Breed Series Companion
Edge of Dawn
Marked by Midnight (novella)
Crave the Night
Tempted by Midnight (novella)
Bound to Darkness
Stroke of Midnight
Defy the Dawn
Midnight Untamed
Midnight Unbound (novella)
Claimed in Shadows
Midnight Unleashed
. . . and more to come!

Hunter Legacy Series
(Midnight Breed Spinoff)
Born of Darkness (forthcoming)

Dragon Chalice Series
Heart of the Hunter (FREE eBook)
Heart of the Flame
Heart of the Dove
Dragon Chalice Boxed Set

Warrior Trilogy
White Lion's Lady (FREE eBook)
Black Lion's Bride
Lady of Valor
Warrior Trilogy Boxed Set

Lord of Vengeance

Midnight Unleashed

A Midnight Breed Novella

By Lara Adrian

1001 Dark Nights

EVIL EYE
CONCEPTS

Midnight Unleashed
A Midnight Breed Novella
By Lara Adrian

1001 Dark Nights
Copyright 2017 Lara Adrian, LLC
ISBN: 978-1-9459-2049-3

Foreword: Copyright 2014 M. J. Rose
Published by Evil Eye Concepts, Incorporated

Acknowledgments from the Author

I am so excited to once again be part of the 1001 Dark Nights collection with this new novella in my Midnight Breed vampire romance series. Thank you to Liz Berry, MJ Rose, Jillian Stein, and the rest of the creative, marketing, and editorial teams at Evil Eye Concepts for the incredible vision and enthusiasm you bring to each release in the collection. It's a pleasure to be working with all of you!

To my amazing readers, thank you for your continued support and for joining me on yet another adventure within the Midnight Breed story world. I hope you enjoy Trygg and Sia's story, and all the rest still to come.

Happy reading!

Love, Lara

Sign up for the 1001 Dark Nights Newsletter
and be entered to win a Tiffany Key necklace.

There's a contest every month!

Go to www.1001DarkNights.com to subscribe

As a bonus, all subscribers will receive a free
1001 Dark Nights story
The First Night
by Lexi Blake & M.J. Rose

One Thousand and One Dark Nights

Once upon a time, in the future…

*I was a student fascinated with stories and learning.
I studied philosophy, poetry, history, the occult, and
the art and science of love and magic. I had a vast
library at my father's home and collected thousands
of volumes of fantastic tales.*

*I learned all about ancient races and bygone
times. About myths and legends and dreams of all
people through the millennium. And the more I read
the stronger my imagination grew until I discovered
that I was able to travel into the stories… to actually
become part of them.*

*I wish I could say that I listened to my teacher
and respected my gift, as I ought to have. If I had, I
would not be telling you this tale now.
But I was foolhardy and confused, showing off
with bravery.*

*One afternoon, curious about the myth of the
Arabian Nights, I traveled back to ancient Persia to
see for myself if it was true that every day Shahryar
(Persian:* شهريار*, "king") married a new virgin, and then
sent yesterday's wife to be beheaded. It was written
and I had read, that by the time he met Scheherazade,
the vizier's daughter, he'd killed one thousand
women.*

*Something went wrong with my efforts. I arrived
in the midst of the story and somehow exchanged
places with Scheherazade — a phenomena that had
never occurred before and that still to this day, I
cannot explain.*

*Now I am trapped in that ancient past. I have
taken on Scheherazade's life and the only way I can
protect myself and stay alive is to do what she did to
protect herself and stay alive.*

*Every night the King calls for me and listens as I spin tales.
And when the evening ends and dawn breaks, I stop at a
point that leaves him breathless and yearning for more.
And so the King spares my life for one more day, so that
he might hear the rest of my dark tale.*

*As soon as I finish a story... I begin a new
one... like the one that you, dear reader, have before
you now.*

Chapter 1

Tamisia stood over the crib and stared down at the plump little form beneath the pink blanket. So precious and innocent. So tenderly mortal. Sia had never given human life more than a passing thought in all her centuries of existence. Now, nothing meant more to her than the protection of this mortal soul and the others under her care at the women's shelter in Rome.

Reaching out, she gently touched her fingertip to the crown of gossamer curls that sprouted from the infant's head. Sia smiled. Angelina was the baby's name, little angel, and it fit. That silken hair, the chubby pink cheeks, and sweet cherub's mouth. Being around this kind of fragile innocence every day for the past month had been a gift, a reminder that even among the bleakest of situations, there was still hope. There was purpose, a reason to get up each morning and greet the sun, things Sia hadn't expected to find again, least of all among mankind.

Some days, if just for a moment or two, she could almost forget the circumstances that had brought her here in the first place.

Almost.

It had been just six weeks since her staggering fall from grace and resulting banishment from the Atlantean colony that had long been her home. Not even a blink of time for one of her kind. The pain was still fresh. So was her shame.

Having real, important work to do helped.

Feeling useful was the only thing keeping her sane when everything else she was had been stripped away from her—through no one's fault but her own.

The image of Elyon's too-handsome face came floating into her mind, bringing with it a second, gruesome image that made her throat constrict with nausea. For as long as she lived, she would never be able to purge the memory of her friend and fellow Atlantean council member Nethilos's murder. Nor would she ever forgive herself for the price of her ignorance when it came to placing her trust in the wrong man.

Before the swell of grief and regret became too much, she shoved away thoughts of the colony and friends she would never see again. Sia wasn't accustomed to feeling emotional weakness, let alone giving in to it. And dammit, she wasn't about to start now.

Her new life was here, in this crowded, often brutal city in this foreign, mortal world.

It was a penance to be sure, but seeing children like sweet Angelina resting safely, peacefully under her care smoothed some of the edge of her melancholy. Her work here mattered. And it was enough, Sia told herself.

With little hope of ever being welcomed back to the colony and her own people, this new life would have to be enough.

Removing her hand from the baby's crib, Sia glanced across the darkened room to where the baby's twenty-year-old mother, Rosa, slept on the narrow bed. The pair had come to the shelter two days ago, alone and scared. Fortunately for Rosa, she bore none of the bruises or broken bones that were all too common among the shelter's other desperate arrivals, but there was no mistaking the terror in the young woman's eyes when she came to beg safe harbor for her and her baby. She was a shy thing, barely giving eye contact to anyone since she arrived, never mind divulging the sordid details of her life or the abuser who'd sent her running to the sanctuary.

Then again, trust, once broken, was not an easy thing to give.

Sia understood that all too well herself.

She blew out a sigh and backed silently out of the room, closing the door behind her. With the rest of the shelter's charges asleep or settling in for the night, Sia picked up a basket of towels and blankets that needed washing and carried it downstairs, the rope of her long blonde braid bouncing against the backs of her thighs with each step.

As she walked into the kitchen on her way to the laundry room, her sole coworker and the founder of the private sanctuary glanced up from a stack of papers on the table.

"You don't need to do that, Tamisia." Phaedra's chestnut brows knit over pale gold eyes. "Please, let me take that for you."

When the beautiful brunette rose from her chair to help, Sia shook her head. "It's all right. I enjoy the work. Continue with what you're doing."

She didn't miss Phaedra's small bow of acquiescence. It was an automatic response that the other woman was still learning to curb, especially around others. No one else in the shelter knew of Sia's unusual origins, let alone the lofty heights from which she had tumbled as one of her people's vaunted elders.

Phaedra knew because, like Sia, she was also Atlantean, one of very few who lived among mankind instead of their own. Unlike Sia, however, Phaedra's life outside the realm had not been forced upon her. She had fallen in love with a mortal man in Rome decades ago, then decided to remain in his world even after death had taken him from her.

And, unlike Sia, Phaedra wasn't banished. She could go home if she wanted. All she had to do was call upon the small silvery orb of Atlantean crystal that dangled from the leather thong around her wrist and Phaedra could teleport back where she belonged. In fact, the crystal's power could carry an Atlantean anywhere they wished; they needed only to concentrate and imagine the place in their mind.

Sia caught herself staring at her friend's wrist, a pang of longing in her breast. Even if her own crystal hadn't been taken away by her fellow council members at the colony, there was likely nothing she could do to redeem herself and persuade them to allow her to return.

Phaedra smiled gently, a wordless acknowledgment of Sia's loss. Then she folded her hands in her lap as if to remove the visual reminder. "It's been a long day. I was thinking I'd cap it off with a cup of hot cocoa and some of the cinnamon biscotti Louisa baked this morning. Would you like to join me after you put those things in the wash?"

Sia nodded. "I'd love to."

"Great. I'll put the kettle on."

Things had been hectic at the shelter, but it had been a good day, even a great one. They'd welcomed three new families into the sanctuary, put a roof over seven heads, and hot food into hungry mouths. The fact that every one of the transitions had gone smoothly and there hadn't been some violent cretin banging on the door demanding to see "his woman" as the new arrivals got settled had to be some kind of record.

Now, at just after midnight, the house was blessedly quiet. No infants squalling or sounds of muffled weeping from the newcomers. Sia let the silence wrap around her like a blanket as she finished in the laundry room and returned to the kitchen.

A plate of crunchy biscotti waited in the center of the kitchen table while Phaedra carried two mugs of steaming hot chocolate over from the stove. "I can't thank you enough for agreeing to come and help out here at the shelter, Tamisia. I don't know how I would've managed without you these past weeks."

"I'm the one who should be thanking you." Sia took one of the mugs from her friend and gently blew at some of the steam. "I'd have gone mad already without something to keep me busy and a comfortable place to stay."

"Comfortable?" She laughed softly. "Now you're only being polite. The house hardly ever quiets down and that tiny attic bedroom you're in upstairs is hardly what you're used to." Her gaze turned wry as she passed the plate of biscotti across the table. "Or was your brief stay with the Breed warriors of the Order so bad it makes this seem like an improvement?"

Sia scoffed at the reminder of how she'd first arrived in Rome. The terms of her exile had placed her in the care of the Breed, a blood-drinking race of beings who had long been her people's primary, most dangerous enemy. Now the Order and the colony were dancing around a tenuous truce in order to unite against a greater enemy.

Sia wasn't sure the partnership could ever work, let alone last. Her kind and theirs were too different, polar opposites, in fact. Atlanteans thrived on light and cherished peace. The Breed ruled the darkness and fed off bloodshed, violence in their very nature.

"Two weeks among those heathens was more than enough." Sia dipped the edge of her biscotti into her cocoa. "Anything would be an improvement over that."

Although to be fair, not all of the Breed were heathens. In the Order's Rome command center, she had been treated kindly enough. In particular, by the group's leader, Lazaro Archer, and his Breedmate, Melena. Most of the other warriors and their mates had been welcoming, too, if not a little curious about the disgraced Atlantean suddenly thrust upon them as an uninvited guest.

Only one warrior, a surly, menacing behemoth of a male named Trygg, looked at her as if she were the enemy in their midst. He'd barely uttered a word around her the entire time she was there. Not that she had wanted him to. Some of the other warriors' mates had disclosed to her that Trygg had been an assassin for many years before he came to the Order. Not by his own will, but as part of an infamous training program created by a madman named Dragos.

Trygg certainly looked the part of a killer. Sia had been away from the command center for a month, yet the memory of his rugged, scarred face, shaved head, and cold, disapproving dark eyes still sent a wave of unease all the way into her bones.

Yes, anything was an improvement over spending another minute under the same roof with him.

Phaedra took a sip from her mug, smiling as she set it down. "Well, I'm grateful that you're here, Tamisia. You were wonderful with the children today, especially Angelina. I think her mama likes you too."

"Really?" Sia couldn't hide her surprise. "How can you tell? Rosa is so meek and quiet."

Secretive, she wanted to say, but held her observation back.

"Rosa is a shy one," Phaedra agreed, "but that could change in time. We have no idea what she's been through."

"She hasn't opened up to you either?"

Phaedra shook her head. "Not yet. But I did see her talking with one of the other mothers today, so I'm hopeful that she'll eventually come out of her shell a bit."

A small thump sounded above their heads. It wasn't entirely out of place to hear movement in the house, but something about it— something about the abrupt way it went silent immediately afterward— made Sia's veins go cold.

"Probably just someone getting up to find the bathroom," Phaedra whispered.

"Probably," Sia replied. She had no reason to think otherwise, but every preternatural instinct she had was screaming in alarm. When she glanced at Phaedra, she saw a flicker of the same stark awareness in her golden eyes too. "I'll go take a look."

"Tamisia, the house is completely locked down and secure. All of the alarms are engaged. No one can get in without the whole perimeter lighting up and tripping a dozen sirens."

And yet someone had.

Sia was all but certain of it.

And then, upstairs, a sharp female shriek confirmed her fears. The scream sounded worse than pained. The quiet that followed lasted not even a moment, then a baby started wailing.

"Oh, no." Phaedra went chalk white. "That's coming from Rosa and Angelina's room."

Sia nodded, grim. No wonder the young mother had seemed so afraid when she arrived a couple of days ago. Her nightmare was far from over. By the awful sounds of it, the man Rosa was running from had decided she wasn't getting away so easily.

Cold dread swept her, seeping into her marrow.

The whole house was coming awake now, vibrating with confusion and terror.

All Sia heard was the piercing wails of the innocent little baby she'd left sleeping so peacefully just a short while ago.

Dammit, no.

Hot rage replaced the chill and her vision blurred into a red haze.

"Stay here, Phaedra. Call for help."

"Tamisia, what will you do?"

She didn't know exactly. There was no time for a plan. She only knew she had to act.

Without answering, she raced for the stairs, pausing only long enough to issue a sharp command to her friend. "The police, Phaedra. Do it now."

Sia was immortal, inhumanly powerful, but she wasn't a fighter. Never had been. She was a politician, shielded by a contingent of Atlantean guards who would fight at her bidding. But none of that mattered as she flew up the steps and past the open doors and terrified faces of the shelter's other residents.

"Back inside, all of you. Don't come out until I tell you to."

No one balked at her hushed orders. One by one, the frightened women and handful of small children retreated, shutting their doors.

Pausing outside Rosa's room, Sia caught the muffled sound of a gravely male voice behind the door. "It's gotta be here somewhere. Keep looking! Santino said no loose ends."

Suspicion pricked at Sia's conscience. This didn't sound like a violent ex-lover coming back to harm Rosa. This was something else. And no less dangerous.

Sia lifted her foot high and kicked the panel so hard it blasted off the hinges.

She'd anticipated one man when she came upstairs, but inside the room were two. One was crouched inside Rosa's closet, hastily tossing her scant belongings. The contents of her small bureau were already dumped on the floor near him.

The other intruder, a massive male dressed all in black, stood beside Rosa's bed, his back to Sia. Rosa dangled from his grasp around her neck, her bare feet hanging several inches off the mattress. Her petite body was limp, lifeless. Her gentle brown eyes gaped open, blank and unseeing.

"No!" Sia roared, even though she realized it was already too late to save her. "Let her go!"

Grief swamped her along with her rage. She'd failed Rosa. She could not fail Angelina too. The baby's unrelenting cries pierced the room. Sia threw a quick glance to the crib where Angelina writhed and flailed.

At least the child was unharmed. Her wails had been torture when Sia heard them from outside the room. Now they gave her strength and a deadly, furious resolve.

"I said put her down."

Rosa's attacker grunted, swinging his dark, shaggy head around to look at Sia.

Fiery amber eyes glowed like lit coals in his skull. His chuckle was inhuman, unearthly, his lips peeled back in a profane imitation of a smile. And within that smile, enormous fangs glinted in the darkness of the room.

Breed.

Sia swallowed as he pivoted around to face her head-on.

"Okay," he snarled. His rough growl was the voice she'd heard on the other side of the door. "If that's what you want, bitch, I'll put her down."

Barking out a coarse laugh, he threw Rosa to the floor, then kicked her out of his way as if she were nothing. His glowing eyes were wild and unfocused, his body trembling from head to toe. Something about him wasn't right. A strange odor emanated from him, something sickly sweet that made her stomach turn.

She didn't have time to contemplate what her instincts were trying to tell her.

He lowered his head and charged her.

Sia felt a great wave of energy rise up from the pit of her being. It exited through her raised hands in a powerful burst of light and strength. The force of it collided with the Breed male's massive body, sending him crashing against the far wall.

"What the fuck!" The human who'd been preoccupied with Rosa's personal belongings now scrambled to turn around in the open closet, his skinny limbs refusing to cooperate. Planted on his backside amid the contents of Rosa's drawers and handbag, his bleary eyes bulged as he looked from Sia to the behemoth Breed male she'd just knocked cold without laying so much as a finger on him.

Power still thrummed deep within Sia, fueled by her fury.

"Wait!" The man held up one hand in surrender. "None of this is my fault! The bitch should've known better than to run from Santino. Should've known she'd get caught eventually."

As he spoke, Sia saw him fumble with his other hand to grab something from beside him.

She didn't realize it was a gun until he aimed it at her with trembling fingers. Without hesitation, he squeezed the trigger again and again and again.

Chapter 2

Son of a bitch.

It was supposed to be a recon mission, nothing more. Now Trygg was cooling his heels in an alleyway across from an old three-story house near the train station, waiting for the two assholes he'd been tailing to wrap up their apparent breaking and entering so he could resume his surveillance of them.

Or, rather, he *had* been waiting.

Until the moment one of the windows on the second floor lit up with what appeared to be a cosmic explosion of pure white energy. Followed by gunfire.

A lot of gunfire.

"Fuck it."

He emerged out of the shadows and headed for the house.

The Order had specifically instructed him not to do anything to alert Roberto Santino or his crew to his presence during this intel-gathering mission. Trygg had been following Santino's muscle, a Breed male named Franco, for the better part of a week now. In the process, Trygg had two of the three set points pinned into the triangulation formula he'd mapped out and was only a couple more data points from being able to nail Santino's lair down to a quarter-mile radius.

Which meant the Order was as close as they'd ever been to locating and taking down one of the most dangerous drug kingpins of Europe.

That mission was a must-do. There were thousands of garden variety narcotics dealers in the world, both human and Breed, and although the Order would never be able to stop them all, Santino was different. The human made no secret of his hatred for the Breed, and he was indulging in that sentiment by dealing in Red Dragon, the worst thing to hit Trygg's kind since its predecessor, Crimson, some twenty years ago.

Secretly manufactured and only effective on the Breed, Red Dragon was a problem nobody needed. Not when relations with the human population in general were already strained. Add in persistent, growing problems with terror groups like Opus Nostrum, and more recent conflicts with the Atlanteans and their unpredictable queen, Selene, and the dead last thing the Order wanted was an epidemic of blood-crazed Breed civilians raising hell—and inciting panic—in all corners of the globe.

In a word, this situation with Santino was war. And collateral damage was to be expected in any war. Not what the Order wanted, but there were times it couldn't be helped. Trygg knew his mission. His commander, Lazaro Archer, had spelled out the rules of engagement for him in no uncertain terms: Anything that jeopardized the prime objective was *verboten*.

Too bad following rules wasn't Trygg's strong suit.

He stalked across the street, certain this was a bad fucking idea. The cries of a baby that had been faint even with his preternaturally sharp hearing intensified tenfold as he leapt to a small wrought-iron balcony on the second story of the house. Over the wailing of the infant in the next room, sounds of a struggle continued. And as troubling as the racket was, the putrid stench of a Breed male high on Red Dragon made Trygg's own blood boil with rage.

The point of entry he stood at was equipped with a remarkably sophisticated alarm system, but it was no match for his Breed ability. With a silent command, he disabled the sensors and cut the heat registers on the glass before mentally freeing the lock on the balcony doors.

It was the same method Santino's Breed thug had used to let himself and his human companion inside a few minutes ago.

What the hell business did they have here?

And where had that blast of white light come from?

He'd have to sort all of that out later. Right now, he needed to neutralize the situation inside the house before things went any further sideways.

A fresh chorus of screams went up as he pushed open the glass doors and slipped inside what he realized now was another bedroom in the house. One occupied by three women of varying ages, all of them clad in nightshirts or robes, huddled together and shrieking at him in terror.

He scowled at the fearful gaggle of females, a response that only made them scream louder. Shit. He knew he was a frightful sight just based on his size and width alone. With his shaved head and the jagged scar that dug deep into the flesh of his left cheek from below his eye to his squared jaw, his looks bordered on nightmarish.

His fangs didn't help, he was sure. The points dug into his tongue as he glowered at the trembling women. "Be quiet. I'm not here to hurt you."

It was a feeble attempt to reassure them, but they were beyond reasoning anyway. And he had neither the skill nor the time to try.

On a snarl, he touched the forehead of the woman nearest to him. "Sleep," he commanded her, putting her into an instant trance.

The two others went down just as swiftly.

Of all the weapons at his disposal, using his Breed ability to manipulate someone's mind was the one he employed the least. In fact, he hated having to use it. As a former Hunter, raised in captivity and trained to kill by a madman named Dragos, Trygg knew what it was like to be controlled, to be forced into doing something at another's will.

For the first fourteen years of his life, he'd been enslaved to the brutal program, compelled to obey through ruthless conditioning and an ultraviolet collar that would have obliterated him if he'd refused any command.

But Dragos was only the first of Trygg's masters.

The last of them had sliced his face wide open—just before he killed her.

Trygg shook off the old memories as an animal roar shook the walls from the room next door. Franco was a sadistic individual in general, but if the Breed male was hopped up on Red Dragon tonight, Trygg hated to think of the violence he was capable of now.

Death and gun smoke clung to the air in the hallway. There was something else in the air too. Something peculiar, like the scent of a recent thunderstorm.

The door to the neighboring bedroom had been smashed off its hinges. From inside, the infant continued to cry. Trygg leapt over the broken panel and into the midst of a scene he never would have imagined.

Three unmoving bodies lay on the floor. A human woman, crumpled like a broken doll beside the narrow bed. Another human, a scrawny male with greasy hair and the sallow face of a crack addict, sprawled in a dead slump inside the open closet as if a great gale force had blown him there.

And the third—the biggest shock of all—Santino's man Franco, lying prone on the floor where he'd been taken down by the woman who stood over him, her long legs straddling his body from behind. The tall, slender blonde held the immense Breed male's head gripped between her hands, giving his neck a final crunching twist just as Trygg stepped inside the room.

"Holy fuck."

She whirled around at the sound of his low voice, her beautiful face a mask of fury, sky-blue eyes fierce with killing fire that all but dared him to test her. A bullet had grazed her shoulder during the struggle, opening a tear in the thin material of her light gray T-shirt. Bright red blood stained the fabric, making his fangs throb in Pavlovian response as he watched the wound slowly heal itself.

His stunned gaze traveled downward, to where the centers of her palms held an unearthly glow. Energy pulsed there, banked but unmistakably strong. He supposed that explained the lightning blast he'd witnessed from outside.

Trygg's mind reeled at the evidence of her unleashed power. But equally astonishing was the fact that he knew this woman.

"Ah, Christ," he snarled as his irritated gaze lifted once again to her face. "You gotta be shitting me."

Tamisia the Atlantean.

Her expression registered recognition too. And plenty of haughty disdain. "What are you doing here?"

He grunted. "I could ask you the same thing."

"I work at the shelter. I live here."

This was where she'd ended up? Working at a women's shelter in one of the roughest areas of the city? Trygg wouldn't have guessed that of the elegant, icy immortal in a million years.

She looked different from when he'd last seen her. Slimmer, her golden skin more pale than luminescent. Her eyes, despite being filled with battle rage, seemed even more haunted than before. Most of her white-blonde hair had come loose from a long braid at her back. It hung in a wild tangle around her, its distinctive single streak of iridescent gold along the left side of her face hanging limp and dulled.

Not that any of these changes diminished Tamisia's otherworldly beauty.

Trygg hadn't cared enough to ask for details about her at the time she'd arrived in Rome, but rumor had it that she'd betrayed her own kind, causing the death of a fellow Atlantean council member. A month and a half ago, he'd helped Lazaro Archer bring Tamisia to the command center as some kind of diplomatic gesture between the Order and her people, but that was as far as Trygg's interest in her had gone.

Or so he'd told himself for the two weeks the female had been underfoot at headquarters.

She'd been a distraction to him from the moment he first set eyes on her. A nuisance he'd been eager to lose when she abruptly left the Order's safekeeping a month ago to make her own way in the city. Trygg hadn't asked where she had gone. He hadn't wanted to know.

He sure as fuck didn't want to be standing in front of the female now, in the middle of a surveillance mission gone all to hell.

Thanks mostly to her.

She seemed anything but concerned with the fact that he was even in the room. Hurrying over to the crib, she collected the squalling baby into her arms. Holding her like precious, fragile glass, she quieted the worst of the infant's cries with soft murmurs and gentle strokes along the child's trembling back.

Trygg ran a hand over the stubble on his shaved head, then exhaled a gruff curse as he assessed the damage to his night's objective. Franco was as dead as he could be. Trygg should have forgone the tail tonight and simply squeezed the Breed male for information. Now Franco was useless to anyone. The Order would have to start all over with a new mark inside Santino's operation. It could take weeks, even months.

"Do you have any idea what you just did, female?"

"Yes." When he glanced at Tamisia, her chin hiked up a notch. "I dispensed justice. Unfortunately, not quickly enough to save Rosa."

Trygg followed her sober gaze to the strangled female near the bed. Rosa looked to be barely out of her teens and no threat to anyone, least of all the pair of assholes who'd broken into the house tonight. He could hear the grief in the Atlantean's soft voice when she spoke about the young woman, but Tamisia didn't shed a tear. In fact, she straightened her shoulders, looking even more determined as she gently stroked the baby's back.

"Tell me what happened."

"The human male was searching her belongings when I kicked in the door. The other one, the bloodsucker, had a hold of her by the throat. He'd already wrenched the life from her in front of her child by the time I got up here. Then he threw her down over there as if she were rubbish."

Her voice shook a bit, not with fear or shock, but with loathing. Trygg only had to look at Franco's big, broken body and snapped neck to understand that her fury tonight must have been off the charts. The Breed and the Atlanteans had been enemies for the longest time, and this brutal attack on a young woman only seemed to fortify Tamisia's animosity toward Trygg and all of his kind.

But Tamisia's feelings were none of his concern. He was more interested in what she'd just divulged about the attack. He glanced at the closet and the upturned drawers and emptied backpack.

"What were they looking for?"

"I don't know."

Trygg walked over and moved some of the scattered clothing and other personal effects with his boot. He didn't see anything of interest. Whatever Franco and his companion were searching for, it didn't appear that they'd found it.

And now Trygg had another wrinkle to smooth in his already fucked-up mission.

No. Make that two.

Sirens sounded in the streets outside, growing louder by the moment. The distinctive whine signaled the pending arrival of the Joint Urban Security Taskforce Initiative Squad, a police force comprised of humans and Breed officers.

"You called JUSTIS?"

She nodded, still cradling the baby in her arms. "My friend who runs the shelter called them. I told her to when we realized someone had broken into the house."

"Fuck." Bad enough his best chance of getting a firm lock on Santino was currently sprawled on the floor with his head nearly twisted off like a bottle cap. Lazaro Archer would be plenty pissed off to hear that newsflash. Hell, Trygg would probably have to answer to D.C. headquarters and the Order's founder, Lucan Thorne, too. About the only thing that would make the night any worse was having to explain to JUSTIS what a member of the Order was doing standing in the middle of a multiple murder scene.

He and his fellow warriors already had a reputation as merciless vigilantes with a habit of enforcing law and order whenever and however they saw fit. Relations with mankind in the past twenty years since the Breed had been outed to them were strained enough without the situation here adding fuel to the fire.

And besides, rumor had it that Roberto Santino had a fair share of the city's police force on his payroll.

He could trance the human officers as soon as they showed up and scrub their minds of all memory of what they found here, but that wouldn't work on the Breed members of the squad. Nor could he erase the record of the emergency call for help that had come from this house. The wheels were already in motion here, and Trygg was going to have to deal with the fallout as best he could.

He looked at Tamisia, standing there with a self-healed gunshot wound and palms still pulsing like embers as she held the quieted infant in her arms. Her regal, ethereal beauty called attention under normal circumstances. After what she'd done tonight, there would be no mistaking her for anything as mundane as human.

Which meant he wasn't the only one who'd have a lot of explaining to do once the law arrived on the scene.

"The cops will be here soon. You'd be wise to avoid them. I doubt this is the way you or any other Atlantean would want to go public to the humans for the first time."

Her face blanched. She looked at the carnage she'd left—carnage no mere mortal was capable of—and true worry flickered in her brilliant blue eyes. "What shall I do?"

"For starters, lose those ruined clothes. There's going to be a lot of questions about what went down in here. Aside from the fact you took out two intruders single-handedly without any trace of a weapon, it'd be damn hard to explain the blood and the lack of a bullet wound where you've obviously been shot tonight."

"Then what are we going to tell the officers when they get here?"

"Not *we*, Tamisia." Trygg bared his fangs in a smile he knew was far from friendly. "You're going to stay out of my way and let me handle this. That's not a request."

The flat line of her lips said she didn't appreciate him telling her what to do, but he gave her points for not arguing with him. In fact, despite his general distaste for females and all the trouble that followed them, the memory of Tamisia standing over Franco's dead body like an unearthly, avenging angel made his cock buck hard behind his zipper.

Not gonna happen.

He ground his molars against the desire that stirred, unwelcome, inside him. "Go. Take the baby out of here and keep the other women away too. I'll go down and wait for the police."

Tamisia stared at him, her head tilted with growing suspicion. "Tell me what's really going on. You knew those men, didn't you?"

"Go, Tamisia. Far as you or anyone else is concerned, this is the Order's business now."

At first he thought she would ignore him. But as the sirens blared in the street outside the house and flashing red and blue strobes lit up the darkness, some of her resistance ebbed.

Finally her ice-blue eyes released him. Tucking the baby against her, she strode out of the room, her spine as straight and stubborn as a queen's.

Trygg made a focused effort not to watch the way her hips and curved backside swayed with each long stride. Ignoring the kick of his veins and the pulse that throbbed in both his emerging fangs and the stiffness at his groin was more struggle than he wanted to admit.

When Tamisia's light footsteps retreated out of earshot, he exhaled the curse he'd been holding and rubbed his palm over his clenched jaw.

Time to get to work.

Chapter 3

Two hours later, Sia stood at the front door and watched the law enforcement vehicles quietly roll away from the house. The ambulances carrying Rosa's body and those of her assailants had departed for the medical examiner a few minutes earlier.

The JUSTIS officers had stayed in Rosa's room for a long time, talking with Trygg and processing the scene. It had taken all the patience Sia possessed to simply wait downstairs with Phaedra and the shelter's residents while the officers did their work and carried out a bag of evidence from Rosa's room.

Sia and Phaedra had been questioned only briefly by one of the human officers, both of them asserting to him that they had called for help as soon as they heard the ruckus upstairs and had been too afraid to do anything more—just as Trygg had privately instructed them to do in the moments before he went outside to meet the arriving squad cars.

Then Sia had dutifully kept her distance from the police and their investigation. Not out of any obedience to the Breed warrior or the Order he served, but out of loyalty to Phaedra and the rest of their people.

Trygg had been right about one thing. She didn't want to be the one who shattered the secrecy that had kept the Atlantean realm hidden as pure myth for centuries upon centuries. She'd already failed the council and her friends in the colony once. She wasn't about to do it again.

As distant a dream as it was that she might one day win back her place among her people, she clung to that small hope. She would never risk even deeper disgrace by giving the humans a reason to suspect she was anything other than human.

Or that there were others like her, both the ones living quietly among man and Breed, as Phaedra was doing, and the hidden populations who lived behind the veil of the colony and in the greater realm ruled by the Atlantean queen, Selene.

Mankind was quick to alarm and slow to trust. After twenty years of coexisting in the open with the Breed, war between the two races remained a constant threat. There might never come a time when the humans were ready to learn they shared their small planet with yet another immortal, otherworldly faction.

"Everyone's exhausted and gone back to their rooms for the night," Phaedra said as she came up beside her. Her ageless face was troubled, sober with grief. "I've moved the baby into my quarters for now. Poor little Angelina. Can you imagine being left without a mother at such a tender age?"

Sia blinked slowly and shook her head, regret tight in her breast. "I'm sorry I wasn't able to save Rosa," she whispered for her friend's ears alone. "I got there too late."

Phaedra's hand came to rest lightly on her back. "It's not your fault, Tamisia. For pity's sake, you weren't the one who killed her. Those awful men did."

Sia nodded, but her thoughts were grim, her mind troubled—not only by the death of an innocent woman, but by the fact that one of the Order's warriors had been tracking Rosa's attackers for some reason. She could imagine no other reason for Trygg to have been close enough to the shelter when the men broke in.

What did he know about them?

Or was it someone else that had piqued the warrior's interest?

She watched Trygg's immense shape moving through the darkness and across the street. Sia had kept her word to stay out of the way while the police were there, but she had questions that needed answers.

"I'll be right back," she murmured to Phaedra, already opening the door and stepping out after him. "Trygg, I need to talk to you."

He glanced behind him but didn't acknowledge her. Moonlight gleamed on the top of his head as he kept walking, his broad shoulders determined and his long, muscular legs practically chewing up the pavement with each hard stride.

When it became clear that he meant to ignore her, Sia picked up her pace, using Atlantean speed to place herself in front of him before he could take another step.

He stopped abruptly, less than an inch to spare between her breasts and the center of his sternum. She was tall, but he was enormous. She hadn't really stopped to recognize that until now. She'd never been this close to the surly Breed male before. Close enough to feel the heat and power of his body, and to inhale the spicy, dark scent of his skin.

During her brief stay at the Order's command center, she had been too put off by Trygg's menacing demeanor to allow herself to truly look at him for any length of time. Now she couldn't help but study him, realizing beneath the scowl and the severity of the shaved head and jagged facial scar, he was actually handsome. Long black lashes fringed eyes of the deepest shade of sapphire she'd ever seen. His nose was straight and regal, his mouth generously cut, even sensual.

He caught her staring, and the furrow between his dark brows deepened.

She awkwardly cleared her throat. "What did you tell the police?"

"The truth, more or less. I was on patrol, tailing a couple of petty drug pushers to this address. I saw them break into the house. When I heard a woman scream, I decided to take matters into my own hands. Not the first time I've had to explain a couple of dead bad guys to JUSTIS. They seemed to buy it."

"Those men. Is that what they were—drug dealers?"

He stared at her. "You don't need to know anything more than what I told the cops, Sia. Do us both a favor and leave it at that."

"They were searching for something, Trygg."

"So you mentioned."

"Do the police have any idea what it might be?"

"I didn't tell them that part."

Sia gaped. "Why not? Rosa was killed for whatever it was they thought she had. If telling the police about it will help them understand what kind of trouble she was in—"

"The police can't help." Trygg blew out an impatient curse. "And whatever those men wanted from the woman doesn't matter now."

"It matters to me," she insisted.

His dark eyes narrowed and he gave a stiff shake of his head. "This conversation is over. I told you, what happened here is the Order's business. Go back inside and get some rest. Forget about tonight."

She scoffed. "Forget it?"

When he started to move around her, Sia grabbed his arm. Warm, hard muscle clenched beneath her fingertips, sending a shocking heat through her body. She drew her hand away at once, trying to ignore the distressing awareness she felt for a man who infuriated her more and more the longer she knew him.

"You think I will ever forget what I saw tonight? A young woman was murdered, Trygg. A woman I liked. A woman I was responsible for keeping safe. And now an innocent little baby is without her mother. Maybe that's something your cold-hearted kind can simply dismiss, but don't expect me to do the same."

"Yes, Tamisia. That's exactly what I expect." He scowled now, his scarred, sinister face taut with growing irritation and something more difficult to define. "In fact, I'm fucking demanding it. You do not want to be involved in this. So stow your questions and march your fine ass back into that house and stay there."

Her jaw dropped open. No one had ever spoken to her like that in all of her immortal existence. She was an Atlantean elder, one of the highest regarded council members in the colony. At one time, she had even been a confidante to the queen herself.

Was. Past tense, all of it.

Now she was merely a foreigner dropped into the middle of a strange, violent land.

And Trygg had no reason to treat her as anything more.

Still, his heavy-handed, gruff demeanor rankled her. It pissed her off.

Even while she couldn't help noting his unexpected comment about her ass.

She stood her ground, refusing to let him think he could cower her. Agreeing to cooperate with him for the protection of her people was one thing. Turning a blind eye to a cold-blooded murder was quite another.

"I want the answers about Rosa's death even if you don't, warrior."

But Trygg did want answers. She had seen that truth in him earlier tonight and she saw it now too. No matter how hard he was trying to convince her otherwise.

He growled a low curse and took a step away from her. Sia followed him with her gaze.

"Who's Santino?"

Trygg stopped dead in his tracks. When his head swiveled in her direction, his expression was as dark as a thundercloud.

"I heard the Breed male who killed Rosa say the name Santino. He told the other man to keep looking for whatever it was they were after. He said Santino didn't want any loose ends."

"Jesus Christ." Trygg came back, seizing her upper arms in his strong grasp. "You're just telling me this now?"

"I would've told you sooner, but you didn't give me a chance before you all but shoved me out the door of Rosa's bedroom."

He swore again, more vividly this time. He didn't let go of her, and despite the anger in his face, the feel of his hands on her was the thing giving her the deepest unease. She couldn't keep from noticing how immense he was, how powerfully male. Atlantean males were strong and masculine, too, but there was a ruggedness about this Breed male that sent Sia's pulse racing more heatedly than she cared to admit.

"Did you say anything about this to your friend Phaedra?"

"No."

"Good. Don't." He released her, but his grim eyes stayed locked on hers.

"Who is he, Trygg?"

"Someone you don't want to cross." She didn't expect him to offer anything more, but then he exhaled a resigned sigh. "Roberto Santino is the biggest narcotics kingpin in Europe. More recently, he's been dealing in a drug called Red Dragon, a substance that's only effective on my kind. It turns even the most mild-mannered Breed into a bloodthirsty animal."

Sia was loath to imagine what a drug like that could do if it penetrated the Breed the way some others had ruined human lives. "It sounds awful."

"It is. That's why Santino needs to be stopped, and quick. The Order's been after him for weeks, but he's a cagey bastard, elusive as hell. Every time we think we've got a bead on the son of a bitch he manages to dodge us. We know he's got friends in law enforcement, so we've been keeping our intel-gathering covert, our operations as far off the radar as possible."

Sia thought back to Trygg's reaction when he learned the police had been called to the shelter. "Do you think any of the JUSTIS officers who came here tonight are connected to him?"

He shrugged. "Possibly. Hell, it's damn probable."

"I'm sorry," Sia murmured. "I'm sorry that Rosa is dead and I wasn't able to save her. But I'm sorry if my actions tonight have gotten in the way of your mission. Sometimes it feels like everything I touch, I ruin."

Trygg's scowl deepened. "You did what you had to, Tamisia. No one can fault you for that."

"Not even you?"

His brows rose, but he didn't take the bait. "Go inside now. You shouldn't be out here."

Whether he meant outside in general or specifically with him, she wasn't certain. He stepped back from her, putting more than an arm's length between them. Sia told herself the chill she felt was merely the night air, not the forbidding nature of the man whose haunted gaze refused to leave hers.

She waited for him to say something, to tell her good night or to growl that he hoped their paths never crossed again.

But Trygg said nothing.

Aloof and impossible to read, he merely turned and walked away without looking back.

Sia watched him until the inky darkness had swallowed him up.

Chapter 4

As soon as the sun set the next night, Trygg hit the pavement on another solo patrol. He'd been twitchy as hell to get back in the city, not only because Lazaro Archer and Lucan Thorne had both taken a bite out of his ass after the debacle at the shelter last night, but also because Trygg hated the knowledge that every hour Santino was allowed to breathe was another chance for the bastard to peddle more Red Dragon and enslave more members of the Breed population.

Trygg was back at square one on his hunt for Santino's lair, and he had a lot of ground to make up fast.

So why the fuck was he parked in one of the Order's black SUVs down the street from the women's shelter again instead of working new leads?

In a word, Tamisia.

His encounter with her last night continued to nag at him for a host of reasons he had no desire to analyze. Chief among them—or so he told himself—was the fact that Franco and his human cohort had been convinced the dead woman, Rosa, had possessed something they wanted.

Ergo, something Santino wanted.

Trygg didn't think anyone else at the shelter was in any danger from the kingpin or whoever might be tapped to replace Franco in the organization, but that didn't mean he wanted to leave Tamisia and the other females unprotected. The Atlantean could handle herself, he had no doubt. But for the time being, Trygg would make a point of keeping a personal watch on the house and its residents.

Besides, it was only sound reconnaissance to want to know if

Santino or his men had any reason to come sniffing around the place again.

Odds were whatever they'd been looking for had likely been picked up by JUSTIS in their processing sweep of Rosa's room and was locked in an evidence hold somewhere at the main station in the city. Santino surely realized that himself by now as well. And if the bastard had his hooks in anyone at the station, he either had access to the items already or would be making his own plans to get his hands on them soon.

Trygg needed to get there first. Which meant it was time to end this little side trip and start putting his last several hours of research to the test. He'd hacked in and downloaded the building schematics of the station. Unless there had been a major renovation in the past six months, the evidence room was on the basement floor in the northwest corner of the building. All he needed to do was determine the best infiltration plan.

The fastest way would be to go in stealth through a window or a portal on the roof, but that meant having to traverse the whole station from inside in order to get to the evidence cages below ground level. Flashing past the humans with his unearthly speed would be cake, but there was no hope of avoiding being spotted by any one of JUSTIS's Breed officers.

As much as he disliked the risk of walking through the front door, it could be the only way. Hiding in plain sight might be his best method of cover. Unless he could create some kind of diversion big enough to allow him to skate past unnoticed.

He was running various options in his head when he spied Tamisia exiting the shelter. He scowled, every bit of his focus now trained on the woman who'd been on his mind too damn much already.

She stepped out to the street in front of the house where a taxi had rolled to a stop to meet her. Her platinum hair was gathered loosely in a twist at her nape. A creamy silk blouse clung enticingly to her breasts, unbuttoned just far enough to give a tantalizing glimpse of the valley between them. Faded jeans hugged her endless legs and long, lean curves.

Taken at a whole, the look was casual, even unremarkable, yet sexy as hell on Sia.

Trygg's cock more than approved. Arousal stirred like a lick of wildfire, all but trumping his dark and growing curiosity.

What the hell was she up to?

She climbed into the taxi and the car took off. Trygg followed at a covert distance, his veins crackling with suspicion.

He probably shouldn't have been surprised when her ride turned in front of the very place he intended to go tonight.

But yet he was surprised. Confused too.

More to the point, he was pissed.

When she got out of the taxi in front of the JUSTIS building, Trygg killed the engine of the SUV and climbed out. He was in her face before she took the first step toward the station's entrance.

Her light-blue eyes widened. "Trygg."

"Yeah. Me." His own eyes felt molten with his anger. "You lost or something, Sia? Because I thought I made it pretty fucking clear that I didn't want to see you anywhere near this operation."

At least she had the good sense to look nervous as he slowly drank her in, giving her an unrushed head-to-toe appraisal. He couldn't decide if she was dressed for a date or an after-hours deposition with law enforcement. Neither idea sat well with him.

And he damn sure didn't want to acknowledge the jab of possessiveness that made his blood race through his veins. She'd been awakening this uninvited need in him since the night before. Longer, if he had the balls to admit it to himself.

This beautiful, headstrong Atlantean female had put him in a twist from the moment she'd arrived in Rome.

"Come with me."

He didn't give her the chance to refuse. Taking hold of her by the arm, he steered her back to the SUV and into the passenger seat. He got in on the other side and slammed the door behind him.

"Talk, Sia. Right now. What are you doing here?"

He was furious, but she was far from flinching. She held his accusing gaze. "I came here to get some answers. I have a feeling I might find them in some of Rosa's personal effects, but they were collected by the officers last night. I can't rest until I know for sure."

Her boldness was a striking reminder that he was dealing with a preternatural being whose fury could easily match his own. That Sia was as lovely to look at as her power was formidable only made his arousal spike even stronger.

"What did you intend to do, stroll inside JUSTIS's evidence room and take them back?" That essentially summed up his own plan, but he sure as hell wasn't going to cop to that now. "You agreed to stay out of my way, Sia. I thought you understood the seriousness of this situation with Santino."

"Yes, I do understand."

She leaned forward as if she expected to do real battle with him—as if she welcomed it. And damn if that didn't make his fangs throb in his gums with a hunger that went deeper than blood or sustenance.

"But you need to understand something too, Trygg. I don't answer to you. I don't answer to the Order, either. You have a mission to carry out. I respect that. After what you told me about this criminal, Santino, I truly hope you succeed. But that doesn't mean you or anyone else is going to dictate what I can or cannot do. And if I decide to bend to your commands of me, don't think I do it simply because you will it."

Trygg relented with a nod. He wasn't sure if all of this anger and defiance was directed at him or at some other male who had manipulated her to do his bidding. He recalled some talk about her banishment from the colony. Whispers that she had put her faith in someone who had his own treasonous agenda. Sia had been deemed complicit, but it was her affection for the male that had blinded her to the fact that she was being used.

Trygg had some experience with being used too. He had the scars to prove it.

"Those men killed Rosa, Trygg. I want to know why." Sia reached out, putting her hand on his for the briefest moment, her gaze imploring. "I think you owe me that much. Especially when neither you nor anyone else from the Order can guarantee the shelter is safe so long as Santino and his men are still searching for whatever they think Rosa had. So, don't ask me to stand by and let the Order handle a problem that's every bit as much mine as it is yours."

Fuck. She had a point. Not one he was eager to indulge, but he didn't think arguing was going to get them anywhere at the moment.

And he didn't have the time to waste on bickering with her.

If the dead woman had something of worth to Santino—something worth killing for—the Order needed to intercept it. Even if that meant Sia was along for the ride tonight.

He scrubbed his hand over his face. "I pulled the building schematics off the JUSTIS servers this morning. I've got the whole place committed to memory, including the layout of the evidence cages."

Her brows rose. "So, you also intended to come for Rosa's things tonight? What was your brilliant plan for retrieving them? I can hardly wait to hear it."

Her lofty tone should have grated, but instead it only made him want to bait her. "I'm a man of action. I prefer to stay fluid when it comes to plans of attack."

"Ah. I see. Meaning you didn't actually have a plan in mind, either."

He shrugged and she let go of a laugh, the first he'd ever heard from her. With her head smugly tilted and her pretty pink lips parted on a smile, she was a temptation. Trygg had an almost irresistible urge to touch her. To kiss her. The soft fall of her platinum hair around her face made him long to feel it between his fingers. Or draped across his bare skin.

Christ.

Hell, yes, he had a plan in mind. Looking at Sia, he had more plans in mind than he had a right to—most of them centering on her being naked and spread out beneath him. He couldn't remember the last time he'd been in such tight quarters with a female, mainly because he made a point to avoid them except on occasions when he needed an open vein to feed from or a fast, anonymous fuck to take the edge off.

Sitting with Sia in the close confines of the vehicle was wreaking bloody havoc on his senses, to say nothing of his concentration. The best thing he could do for both of them was to get his hands on whatever Santino was after from the dead woman, then get on with the business of hunting down his target. Anything to put a lot of space between himself and Sia.

And the sooner the better.

He pulled a black skullcap out of his jacket pocket and plugged his head into it, pulling the knit hat low onto his brow. "I'm going in. And you're not going anywhere near that building. Understood?"

She started to balk, but his dark glower seemed to actually give her pause. "What are you going to do, Trygg?"

"My fucking job."

She watched him pull the collar of his leather jacket up to cover the Breed *dermaglyphs* that tracked up his neck. When he checked the pair of sheathed daggers that he wore strapped around his torso beneath the jacket, Sia swallowed.

"Do you think you're going to need those?"

"Not if I can help it."

"Trygg, there must be close to a hundred officers in there—many of them Breed. If you get caught, you won't be able to take them all."

His grin felt more like a sneer. "Don't be so sure. You have no idea what I'm capable of. And trust me, Sia, you wouldn't want to know."

She sat back at that bleak admission, dark questions swirling in her uneasy gaze. "It's a busy night at the station. There have been people coming and going the entire time we've been here. So, how do you expect to get inside?"

"Right through the front door." He grunted, closing up his jacket. "Be a hell of a lot easier if I didn't have this face. It tends to get noticed. And not easily forgotten."

Sia didn't laugh at his joke. He wished he hadn't said it now, feeling her studying him, knowing he must seem beastly to a beauty like her. Ordinarily, he'd find solace in his monstrous looks. Caught in Sia's unflinching gaze, he felt exposed. Cut open all over again.

Before he realized what she was doing, she lifted her hand and brushed her fingertips over his scarred cheek. "Promise me you'll be careful, Trygg."

No one had ever asked that of him before. No one had ever cared. Not unless they wanted something in return.

But Sia's eyes were tender on him, her voice sincere. And as unexpected as her touch was against his riddled cheek, he barely held back his groan of pleasure in the instant before she drew her hand away.

Emotions churned, mixing with the desire that was becoming increasingly difficult to contain. He clenched his fists, if only to keep from taking hold of her and dragging her into his arms.

He didn't quite know how to process any of what Sia made him feel, other than to shut it down hard.

"I have a job to do." Opening the driver's side door, he threw her a cold look. "Do us both a favor, Sia. Don't be here when I get back."

Chapter 5

Sia sat in the dark vehicle for only a moment. She watched Trygg stroll casually toward the entrance of the station, her irritation growing with each passing second.

What just happened?

She'd felt the sizzle of awareness that had ignited between them when she touched him, and she knew he had too.

Yet Trygg, a behemoth of a male whose lethal glower and deep, gravel-rough voice made even the warriors of the Rome command center stand a little straighter when he was around, had practically scrambled to get away from her.

Right after ordering her to be gone when he got back.

She knew if she left she would never see him again. He would make sure of that now.

Because somehow, in spite of the fact they couldn't seem to avoid locking horns or struggling for the upper hand, she and Trygg had connected. And it had scared him.

It scared her, too, especially when she was still licking her wounds from the last time she'd allowed herself to get close to a man.

But Sia wasn't the type to run.

She preferred to face her problems head on.

And the biggest problem she had right now was the stubborn, overbearing Breed male who seemed to think he had to take on the world and all of its troubles single-handedly.

Sia stared daggers into the back of his covered head as he fell in behind a cluster of bikers who were just entering the station. Even with his shoulders hunched and his hands shoved into his pockets, he stood out like a tree among shrubs.

Not that he couldn't handle whatever happened once he got inside. She trusted his skills were every bit as stealthy and lethal as his reputation proclaimed them to be. But that didn't mean she wasn't anxious.

He'd been gone only a few seconds and the wait was already killing her.

"Dammit."

She shook her head on another exhaled curse, then hopped out of the vehicle. Her plan for how she might help him took shape in her mind as she walked the first few steps over the dark pavement. Reaching up, she vigorously mussed her hair, then tore her sleeve loose at the shoulder. For good measure, she also ripped one side of her blouse wide open, exposing her lace bra and a fair amount of bare skin.

By the time she neared the station in her disheveled state, she had managed to make tears well in her eyes and force her breathing into a panicked, rapid pant.

"*Aiutami! Aiutami! Per favore!*"

Every head turned as she rushed inside, screaming for help in fluent Italian.

Every head, including the dark one that towered over most of the others in the busy lobby.

She didn't dare look directly in Trygg's direction as she carried on about being attacked just outside the station, but she felt his hard eyes boring into her in the second before she collapsed dramatically on the floor. No less than a dozen officers—Breed and human alike—hurried over to assist her.

She kept up her ruse, using all of the Atlantean allure at her disposal. Just to be safe, she also made sure to show just enough skin to keep her male audience's attention riveted while several officers ran outside to look for her assailant and still more crowded around to offer her water and comfort while she pretended to fade in and out of consciousness.

She didn't know how long to continue with the act. She'd lost sight of Trygg almost immediately and could only hope he'd had enough time to locate the evidence room and retrieve Rosa's belongings as a couple of kind JUSTIS officers helped show her to the ladies' room so she could compose herself enough to file a report of the "assault."

Sia waited in the restroom for several long minutes before peering around the door to find the corridor quieted and empty. Ducking out, she hurried to the nearest side door and made her escape into the adjacent alley.

Trygg was waiting there for her, his scowl firmly in place and his bulky arms crossed over his chest. "Nice work. Very convincing."

"Thank you." She lifted her bared shoulder and offered him a satisfied smile. "It almost seemed too easy. Maybe being Atlantean in this world has its advantages."

He grunted. "Don't ever do something like that again."

He strode away from her, his boots thumping on the pavement, his pace agitated. Sia marched after him. "Why are you upset?"

He wheeled on her, his hands clamping around her biceps in a grip so fierce he shook with it. "I told you not to come inside." He ground out the words, his eyes crackling with sparks that told her just how hot his anger was. "I told you to leave because I don't want to be responsible for you, Sia."

"You're not responsible," she snapped. "I've been taking care of myself for longer than you've been alive. In case you've forgotten, warrior, I'm immortal. If someone wanted to kill me, they'd have to be determined enough to take my head."

"That doesn't mean you can't be hurt," he shot back angrily. "Do you have any idea what I thought when I heard your voice behind me in there? I thought something had actually happened to you. I thought Santino or one of his men—" He broke off on a harsh curse. "Forget it. Doesn't matter what I thought. It was just an act and you played it well."

She blinked, utterly stunned. "You were afraid for me, Trygg?"

"Afraid?" He scoffed, those glowing flecks in his eyes blazing now. "I'm mad as fuck, woman."

His grasp tightened on her arms, almost to the point of pain. When his lip curled back from his teeth, all she could see was the razor-sharp points of his elongating fangs. But as enraged as he surely was with her, his eyes kept darting to her mouth. She watched his nostrils flare, his harsh face as terrifying as she'd ever seen it.

And yet she was certain that the worst this deadly Breed male wanted to do to her right now was kiss her.

Do it, she thought, all but daring him to as she lifted her chin and stared unflinchingly into his fiery, wild eyes. Her heart raced at the idea, her pulse drumming from both leftover adrenaline and the even stronger rush of arousal that spiraled through her as she held Trygg's heated gaze.

After a long moment, he made a frustrated sound in the back of his throat, then his grip fell away. The air between them still pulsed with unresolved desire, but Trygg's face was a mask of indifference now. "We're finished here, Sia. I'll drop you at the shelter on my way back to the command center."

His tone was flat, all business. He'd returned to warrior mode as they'd walked to the waiting SUV, and she should probably be thankful for that. Hadn't she messed up her life enough without adding to it by getting involved with a crude beast like Trygg?

Except he wasn't crude, nor a beast.

And she *was* involved.

Like it or not, they were bound by a common goal—unraveling Rosa's secrets.

"What about the evidence?" she asked once they were seated in the vehicle.

"What about it?"

"Did you get Rosa's things?"

His nod was curt as he started the engine and rolled into the river of evening traffic. "I got them."

"Let me see!" She could hardly contain her excitement. He reached inside his leather jacket and withdrew a bulging large brown envelope. She grabbed it out of his hands and broke the seal. "Have you looked inside?"

"Not yet. After I snatched it, I was too busy wondering if I'd have to save a certain Atlantean's reckless ass."

Sia smirked. "Fine ass, you mean."

He nearly choked, swiveling a confused frown on her. "What?"

"Isn't that what you said last night outside the shelter? I believe you said I had a fine ass."

He scowled, but words seemed to fail him. Sia shrugged, pretending she wasn't taking far too much satisfaction in his flustered reaction. She opened the envelope and reached inside.

"There's not much in here." She carefully spilled the contents into her lap. Rosa's wallet, which contained only a handful of euros and her ID. Her phone. A gold locket on a delicate, broken chain. "I never saw Rosa without this necklace on. It must've fallen off when that bloodsucking monster strangled her."

Trygg glanced at her as they approached a red traffic light. "What about the phone? Power it up. Let's see who she's been talking to recently."

Sia tried, then shook her head. "It's asking for a passcode."

He didn't touch the device, but a small vibration buzzed her fingertips. "Try it now."

"Showing off, vampire?"

He smirked. "You'll know when I am."

The phone lit up in her hands, unveiling the home screen and a photo of Rosa holding Angelina in her arms on a bright, sunny day. The baby was wrapped in a pink blanket, and Rosa's expression was one of pure happiness, captured in the midst of a joyful laugh. Sia traced her finger around the mother and child, her heart squeezing with sadness.

"What do you want me to search for?" she murmured.

"Phone calls, messages. Anyone she communicated with on a regular basis, but also any anomalies. Even a one-off phone number or text could be the lead that will bring us closer to her connection to Santino."

As Sia scrolled through weeks and months of incoming and outgoing calls in the phone's history, she thought back to the photo of Rosa and her baby. "You don't suppose she was involved with him, do you? Santino and Rosa. Could they have been lovers?"

Trygg chuckled as he turned the SUV onto the street where the shelter was located. "Highly doubtful."

"How can you be so sure?"

"Because Roberto Santino prefers men in his bed. The younger the better. He's even paid for boys when it suits him, according to our intel on the sick fuck."

A brutal edge crept into Trygg's rough voice as he relayed that last bit of information. He'd made it no secret that he despised the criminal for his proliferation of Red Dragon and other drugs, but this charge against Santino seemed to resonate someplace deeper in Trygg.

Sia wanted to ask him about it. She wanted to know so much where he was concerned.

But Trygg lived behind steep walls. She was seeing that for the first time tonight. Where before, after she had first arrived from the colony, she had dismissed him as a menacing brute. With his forbidding looks and surly attitude, she had been only too happy to avoid his dark glares and off-putting silence.

Now it just made her want to know more.

As an Atlantean elder, one who had spent all of her long life safely cocooned behind the veil that shielded her kind from violence and bloodshed, the idea that she might be intrigued by one of the Breed—and a warrior besides—would have been laughable. That she could actually be attracted to one of them? Well, that would have been beyond horrifying.

Yet she felt desire and then some for Trygg.

She studied him as he pulled up in front of the shelter.

As soon as they were parked, he pivoted toward her. He held out his hand, the big broad palm open. "I'll take that phone now, Sia. And the rest of those things."

"No." The refusal slipped past her lips before she could stop it. She shook her head. "No. I'm not going to give it up. This evidence belongs to me as much as it does you or the Order."

"Like hell it does."

"I helped you get it tonight and you know it. At least be man enough to admit that—"

He flashed his fangs at her. "Oh, I am man enough, Sia. Man enough for anything you've got in mind."

"You don't frighten me, Trygg. And like it or not, we're in this together."

His expression darkened. "Damn right I don't like it."

"Good. Then at least we agree on something."

She slid the phone and the rest of the contents back into the envelope. Then she hopped out of the vehicle, closing the door on Trygg's vivid curse behind her.

Chapter 6

While he'd sure as hell rather be surrounded by his tech equipment at the command center, Trygg couldn't find much to object to as he followed Sia up an exterior staircase to a private third-floor entrance of the house. As irritated as he was after her power play in the car just now—not to mention her earlier act of defiance that had rattled him more than he cared to admit, even to himself—it was hard to think about much else except the rhythmic sway of her hips as she mounted the old iron steps.

Very hard.

Her long, elegant spine and firm backside were a temptation that stoked a growing heat inside him as he stalked up the climb behind her. Everything male in him burned with desire. Everything Breed in him hungered for her too. If she chanced a look over her shoulder, it would be damn close to impossible to hide the amber lighting his irises or the press of his sharp fangs as they filled his mouth.

Letting her win just now was a mistake he already regretted, but that's where her control was going to end. He'd go inside as she insisted and they'd do a cursory look through the rest of the items they'd brought with them. He would point out something or other so she'd have a bone to chew on, then he'd take everything back to the command center and dig into the meat of the scant evidence alone.

The way he preferred to operate.

He scowled at her when they reached the top of the stairs. "Is this the way you sneak in all the men you bring home with you?"

"Only the surly ones." Her blonde brow arched over her long-lashed eyes. "And to answer the question you really want to ask, I've never brought anyone up here before."

He didn't want to ask that, so why did her answer give him such a healthy stab of satisfaction?

"Come in." She opened the door into a cramped, one-room attic apartment. Trygg stepped inside, feeling like a giant in a dollhouse. The decor was aged and modest, the rug covering rustic wood floors threadbare. An upholstered chair and mirrored dresser stood on one side of the room. On the other was a narrow bed.

Sia walked over and sat on the edge of it, dumping the evidence envelope onto the coverlet. When Trygg didn't budge, she looked at him expectedly. "Are you going to stand over there the whole time? Sit down, Trygg." Her mouth twisted with amusement. "I'm not going to bite you."

Christ.

Just the thought made his cock buck against his zipper. Was the heat on in the room? Suddenly he was too warm, the confined space seeming as tight as a cell. He swiped the skullcap from his head and shrugged out of his leather jacket, setting both on the cushioned chair as he walked over to the bed and sat down beside Sia.

She was already engrossed in the phone once more, paging through the call history and text threads. "Only a few of her messages are recent. It's as if she cut off most of her other ties about a year ago. Oh. What's this one? There's no name attached to the text, just an odd number."

Trygg glanced at the screen. "The phone number it came from has a block on it. People use them when they don't want to be identified."

Sia looked at him pointedly. "This is the only person Rosa communicated with on a regular basis in the past three months. And look—most of these texts came in five days ago. Trygg, Rosa showed up at the shelter two days later."

He leaned closer. "Let me see those texts."

She gave him the phone and he scrolled through the conversation thread. "It's a male. She's careful not to use his name, but she's talking to him about their baby. Sounds like he could be married to someone else."

Sia scoffed. "What a prince."

"A lot of these messages are idle chat." Trygg's jaw tensed as he skimmed a few of the more explicit comments. He was already having enough trouble staying focused on the task at hand with Sia sitting close enough that he could feel the warmth of her body, her sweet scent filling his head with all kinds of dangerous ideas. He cleared his throat and kept scrolling. "A couple of months ago, Rosa thanks him for a gift he gave their daughter, says it's the child's favorite thing. That she can't go to sleep without it. There's a gap in dates between that text and the next one. He's telling her there's a problem on his end and he needs to lay low for a while."

"I'll bet," Sia interjected. "A problem with the wife?"

Trygg smirked and scrolled through a few more messages. "He doesn't elaborate. The next time he contacts her is five days ago. He tells her he's leaving Rome the next day. She's upset, doesn't understand what's going on. He doesn't say, just urges her to take the child and go somewhere else too."

"She didn't take his advice," Sia murmured grimly. "Rosa stayed, and now she's dead."

Trygg nodded. "Which seems to suggest she had no idea about the trouble this man of hers was in. Or that he'd somehow put her into it too."

"The poor girl. She deserved better than that. Better than him."

"What about photos?" Trygg asked.

Sia shrugged. "The only one I saw was on the home screen."

Trygg made a quick check of the galleries. "Everything's been deleted. Or has it?"

With a few taps and swipes and hardware overrides, he managed to break open the cache of deleted photos. Just as he suspected, the majority of the images were ones of Rosa, some with her baby, some of them intimate, meant for her lover's eyes only. He ignored those few out of respect, and because he was searching for something specific.

And there it was.

A selfie she had taken in a sun-filled park. Rosa was pregnant, and seated beside her was a man. He looked a bit old for her, with gray at his temples and shadows under his eyes.

Trygg peered at the human male, zooming in on his face. "Holy shit."

Sia leaned closer. "What is it?"

"I've seen him before." He grabbed his own phone and pulled up a search browser. The news article he was looking for filled his screen. He showed it to Sia.

She glanced at the story and the accompanying photos, then read the Italian headline aloud. "Body of Gianni Tiaggi, Special Investigator for the Guardia di Finanza, recovered from the Tevere near the Vatican on Sunday morning." She looked at Trygg, her lovely face drawn in shock. "Santino had him killed?"

"Considering that the Guardia di Finanza is the agency in charge of investigating international drug trafficking, there's no doubt that Santino had him dealt with. Now we need to figure out what Tiaggi did to cross him, or what he might've had on the bastard that was damaging enough for Santino to have him killed. Maybe that something ended up in Rosa's possession. If it did, she probably didn't even realize she had it."

"What kind of man would jeopardize the mother of his own child like that?"

"A desperate one." Trygg picked up the gold locket. "Didn't you say Rosa was always wearing this?"

"I never saw her without it on."

He tried to open the delicate piece of jewelry, but struggled. His hands were too big, his fingers more accustomed to weapons and technology than fragile, feminine things.

Sia reached for it, her soft touch brushing his knuckles. "Here, let me do that."

Sitting next to her so closely on the narrow mattress was its own kind of hell. Now that she had pressed up even tighter to him as she worked on the locket, it was all he could do to resist reaching out to smooth his fingers through the loose cascade of her platinum hair. She smelled like citrus and fresh sea air, and her body's warmth radiated against him like the heat of the sun. His mouth watered as he breathed her in, his fangs throbbing as they slid out of his gums behind his closed mouth.

"Got it," she blurted, glancing up with a smile as she held the tiny photo frame open to him.

The image was a close-up of the baby's sleeping face, her tiny fist resting against her cheek and wrapped tight around the edge of a pink blanket.

"She's such a sweet child," Sia murmured, gazing at the picture. "It breaks my heart to think of how much she's been through in her short little life."

Hearing the sadness in her voice, Trygg wondered if Tamisia had ever wanted children of her own. Before he could stop himself, a shocking mental fantasy came to life in his head. He and Sia making love. Him planting his seed inside her while he sank his fangs into her creamy throat.

Fuck.

Arousal surged through him, instant and uncontrollable. The erection he'd been fighting all night raged to life, making him shift in discomfort on the bed. He cleared his throat, but nothing could mask the rough edge of his voice.

"Take the photo out, Sia. Maybe there's something behind it."

She nodded and went to work, gently prying it out with her fingernail. She shook her head. "Nothing. Just a photo in a locket. Dammit!"

"We'll find it," he assured her, but he had to admit his own disappointment too. "I'll bring these things back to the command center and the Order will take care of the rest, Sia. Then you can let all of this ugliness go and get on with your life."

Nothing could've prepared him for her bleak, haunted expression or what it did to him inside. "Life as I knew it ended six weeks ago, when my inaction caused the death of a friend and beloved husband and father. I won't stand by and let bad things happen ever again. If I'm willing to do that after everything I've lost, then I should have refused my banishment and begged the colony to kill me."

He let her rant, sensing she needed it. She wasn't a woman to lose control, and the fact that she felt safe enough to do so with him moved him more deeply than he cared to admit.

"Do you miss it? Your old life with your people."

"Every day." She smiled sadly. "But it doesn't matter. I can never go back and I'll never be able to redeem myself to the colony, so I must do it here. I have to do something purposeful with this new life—for myself as much as I want to show my people that I'm not the awful person they believe me to be. I need to prove that I have honor, that I'm worth something."

"You don't have to prove a damn thing to anyone, Sia. You are all of those things already."

She gave him a humorless laugh. "Flattery from you?"

He shook his head. "The truth. I'm just telling you what I see."

Her eyes softened as she looked at him. Before he realized it, her fingers came to light gently on his face, tracing his hideous scar and clamped jaw. "Do you want to know what I see? You are everything I didn't expect. A brave warrior. A man of deep honor and conviction. I see someone who's been hurt very badly and not only survived, but emerged stronger." She stroked his ruined cheek, tender light shining in her eyes. "What did you survive, Trygg? I know your early life was hard. I've heard something about the program you were in—a Hunter, isn't that what you were called?"

"Yes, that's what we were called." He exhaled sharply, but allowed her touch to linger on him for a moment before moving away from her warmth. "What we were was killers. Held like prisoners, treated like animals. Worse than animals. We had one purpose from the time we were born, and that was to deliver death on our master's command."

Sia listened, unflinching. But when she spoke it was with a soft, careful voice. "Why did you stay?"

That answer was as simple as it was final. "I didn't know any other life. None of us did. Even if we had, there was no chance for us to seek it out. If we tried to run, we died. If we disobeyed or showed the slightest defiance or regret during our training, we died."

"But even as children, you and the others must have been strong. Was there no way to overtake this madman and save yourselves?"

"Dragos planned for that possibility. Every boy in the program was fitted with an unbreakable ultraviolet collar that would detonate if tampered with…or whenever Dragos ordered our termination." Trygg's hand came up to his neck in reflex. "Sometimes I swear I can still feel the cold black polymer against my skin."

Sia's gaze lowered, her breath escaping on a shallow sigh. "He sounds like the worst kind of monster."

"He was," Trygg agreed, recalling too many of the faces of his brothers in the program, many of whom had served as horrific lessons to Trygg and the other boys that there was no escaping Dragos or the UV noose he'd fitted them with as soon as they could walk. "Dragos trained us to be monsters too. He trained us well."

Sia said nothing for a long moment. "And it was the Order who finally freed you?"

He nodded. "I owe them my life. I'd lay it down for any one of my warrior brethren."

"That kind of loyalty is a rare gift," she murmured, her expression distant and regretful, as if she hadn't ever seen that kind of faith in anyone herself. "How did they save you, Trygg?"

"When they defeated Dragos, an Order warrior named Gideon found a way to remotely disable the lock codes on the Hunters still in the lab. Like me, most of them were young boys. I was fourteen."

"So, did you join the Order immediately?"

"No. I made my own way in the States for a while. It wasn't until I arrived in Italy that I sought out the Order and offered my life in service to them."

He chose to stop there, telling his history with an utter lack of inflection, precisely how the program had taught him to be. No emotions. No need for care or affection. Just cold, machine-like efficiency. No Hunter came out of the program without a heart as cold and sharp as a blade.

If he didn't watch himself, a woman like Tamisia could smooth those sharp edges.

Make him weak.

Hell, she already was. How else could he explain the fact that he had let her hijack his mission tonight? Now he was sitting on her bed with an envelope of evidence spread out before him and questions badly in need of answers, yet all he could think about was the pleasure of Sia's touch. Her expressive, sky-blue eyes filled with tender emotion…and desire.

"What happened to the Hunters who were freed?"

He shrugged his shoulder. "I'm only aware of a handful. One of them, named Scythe, lives with his mate Chiara here in Italy."

"Is he as big and grumbly as you?" Sia asked, her pretty mouth curving.

Trygg chuckled. "He was. Chiara has gentled him somewhat, but I'm sure my half-brother is still a pain in her ass."

Sia laughed. She gazed at him, tilting her head in amusement. "And is Scythe as handsome as you?"

Trygg felt his face harden into a stony mask. "Don't play me, Tamisia." His low voice came out like a lash. "I'm well aware of the way I look, and I'm not as easily fooled as the men fawning at your feet back at the JUSTIS station."

"I'm not playing you." She sounded utterly sincere, even stung. "Do you think the scar makes you ugly? It doesn't. Not to me. Only someone's actions can make them ugly, Trygg."

He took no comfort in that opinion. "Then if you knew everything I've done in my life, you'd think I was hideous."

"So tell me, Trygg. Why not let me decide for myself?"

He turned his head on a curse. "I didn't come up here to talk about me."

"Then why did you come?" Her fingers were at his chin, drawing his gaze back to her. "You could've just as easily taken that envelope out of my hands. You could have walked away tonight like you threatened to do, but you didn't. Why not?"

It took more control than he thought possible not to yank away from her light grasp and head for the door. But that would only confirm his worst fear—that this woman was getting under his skin. That she was getting perilously close to his heart.

"Don't push me, Sia."

She shook her head. "I think a push is exactly what you need."

Without warning, she took his mouth in a hard, hot kiss.

Chapter 7

He moaned sharply as their mouths came together. His hands were at her shoulders, his fingers like iron, so immensely strong. For a moment Sia thought for certain he was going to shove her away.

She had overstepped her bounds by kissing him. She knew that. She might have even lost her mind, pushing a dangerous Breed male like Trygg. A Hunter. A cold, emotionless assassin.

But he felt anything but cold.

He didn't feel emotionless, either.

He was hot and wild against her lips, as powerful as a storm. His hands came up to cage her face as he took their kiss deeper. She opened to his tongue, eager for the invasion.

She was on fire too. For this killer with the haunted, dark eyes. This Breed male who was like nothing she'd ever known before.

As he kissed her, all she felt was need for the man who made her crave his darkness the way she needed light—for strength and nourishment, for survival at its most elemental.

She was immortal, as formidable as any Breed, but she had never felt more delicate and small than she did now with him. And she marveled at the feeling, savored it.

Liquid fire shot through her and she groaned as her nipples tightened into stiff peaks. Primal, unadulterated power flowed from him, his strength and vitality drawing her in, making her ache with a desire so consuming it astonished her.

He drew back then, his eyes blazing with fiery amber, his fangs enormous between his parted lips as his breath rushed out of him, scraping and raw. "It's been too long for me, Sia. And the way you look…so fucking beautiful. Christ, the way you feel."

He broke off on a groan, bringing his hands to her shoulder and the ripped sleeve of her blouse. He toyed with the frayed edge for a second, then rent it loose, tearing the garment away from her body and pushing her down onto the mattress. Sia gasped at the sudden rush of cool air as her heated skin was exposed to him. But his heat filled the space soon enough, and then his mouth was on her shoulder, her clavicle, the swell of her breast still encased in the lace of her bra.

"You've consumed me since I first saw you," he murmured, his tongue hot and wet on her sensitive skin. He closed his lips over the clasp at the front of her bra, then he caught it between his teeth and bit it open. His moan as he swept the thin fabric away from her was pure male, utterly possessive. "You've been a torment, Sia, but tonight? Fuck. The way I felt when you came into that station looking like someone'd had their hands all over you—"

He bent his head to kiss her breast, taking her tight nipple into his mouth while he reached between her legs to cup her sex through the denim of her jeans.

She writhed at the spike of need that arrowed through her as he suckled hard and caressed her ruthlessly, punishing her with his tongue and teeth and hands. When he finally drew his mouth away and glanced up at her, his pupils were narrow slits, his irises like an inferno of need and something deeper that she could not name.

"Was I worried that something had happened to you?" he snarled thickly. "Hell, yes. Was I pissed when I realized your game? I swear, I wanted to kill you at that moment, Sia. I could've throttled you with my bare hands." He bared his fangs in a threat that made her shiver, though not with anything close to fear. And with every harsh word he growled at her, his hands continued their tender assault on her aching body. "I wasn't prepared for what seeing you like that did to me. Ever since, I can't decide if I want to drive my fist through a wall or my cock into you."

She couldn't curb her desire-drenched smile. "If you're asking me to choose, I'd much prefer the latter."

To prove her point, she reached down to cup his huge erection over the zipper of his pants. The shaft more than filled her grasp, surging even bigger as she stroked him. He uttered her name in a low, otherworldly snarl, then claimed her mouth in a deep, urgent kiss.

Sia reached for the back of his black shirt and dragged it up and over his shoulders, his mouth only leaving hers long enough for her to free him from the clothing. They lay back and kissed some more, his thick thighs straddling her and his hands sliding into her hair, anchoring her in place while he traced the tender skin on the inside of her bottom lip before nipping hard.

She gasped as a bolt of need shot through her, pooling in her core. He tore his mouth away as he reared back to stare at her, his pupils barely visible in the center of so much hot amber light. Breed *dermaglyphs* tracked all over his body and onto his neck. The multi-hued skin markings were like a painting now, his desire for her making the swirls and arcs and tangled vines of patterns surge with motion and pulsating colors.

Sia had never seen anything as magnificent. Every inch of him was dense muscle and firm skin swirling with the strange, alien markings, these living, moving testaments of his need for her. Nothing at all like the sun-kissed, golden skin of her past lovers in the colony, including Elyon, whose fine-hewn physical perfection could have made the angels weep.

No, with his massive build and bulging muscles, Trygg looked more demon than angel. And her hungry eyes couldn't get their fill of him.

"You're glorious, Trygg." She smoothed her fingers over his warm muscles and the stunning *glyphs* that were uniquely his own. "The most incredible man I've ever seen."

His sensual mouth twisted at her praise, but this time he didn't reject it. His breath sawed out of him, his fangs like pearly daggers as he gazed hungrily at her beneath him.

"Beautiful Sia," he said, his hands roaming from her waist to the swell of her hip. Gripping her there, he dragged her against his groin, using his hold to crush their bodies more tightly together. "Have you ever been with a Breed before?"

Although phrased as a question, he meant it also as a warning. One that made her veins throb and the heat gathering in the center of her turn even more molten.

She shook her head. "I've never wanted to be. Now I can't think of anything I've ever wanted more. Just you."

With the press of his hard, thick arousal jutting against her, she moaned, suddenly desperate to get even closer. He leaned over her, tugging hard on her hair as he took her mouth again, his hold tilting her head back on her shoulders, baring her throat to him.

She could feel her pulse pounding there and froze, wondering if he wanted to sink his teeth into her flesh. Some wild, reckless part of her wanted him to. Dared him to. Anything to make this dark, needy pull inside her subside. But no, he only skimmed his lips over her skin, leaving a trail of flames in their wake as he moved lower.

"So damn soft," he muttered on a groan as he scraped along her jawline with the very edge of his fangs. For a second, he pulled back to drink her in with the heat of his molten gaze.

Then he was on her again, this time his hands at her waistband, deftly unbuttoning her jeans, slowly working her zipper down. She helped, wriggling her hips as he slid the material down over her thighs and onto the floor. It was only when he straightened that she realized he'd gotten her panties as well. And now she lay before him naked.

The pulse in his neck hammered like a drum as his gaze traveled over her. He pushed her legs apart roughly and dropped his head down between her spread thighs. A moment later, he was on her, his molten mouth covering her sex as his tongue flicked against the part of her that ached most.

She closed her hands over his stubbled head and held tight, reveling in the feel of his mouth on her. He mastered her pleasure, combining long, sensual strokes with quick, brutal lashes of his tongue over her clit and deep into the cleft of her sex. Then he dipped a finger inside the wet heat of her channel and stars exploded behind her closed eyelids.

Her body erupted into climax, the world going out of focus as wave after wave of ecstasy crashed over her. So quickly, he'd sent her over the edge and now she wanted nothing more than for him to join her.

She reached for him, not caring if she showed him how badly she needed him.

Desperate. That was the only word for how she felt.

She was desperate to feel his length inside her. Filling the space that felt so empty. Making her forget how lonely she had truly been since arriving in this mortal world. How lonely she had been even back home in the colony.

She scrabbled for his belt, her movements unusually clumsy. When she released a frustrated sound, he covered her hands with his, speeding things along. In moments, he was naked. And if Sia had thought him impressive before, the sight of him fully unclothed and unabashedly aroused robbed all of the air from her lungs.

His answering grin held no shame. And why should it? He was

magnificent.

And, at least for right now, he was hers.

"Touch me," he commanded her, as if she needed the direction.

Her hands were already reaching for him, greedy to feel his power in her palms…and in her body.

He groaned, dropping his head back as she stroked him. But he didn't allow her to explore for long. On a snarl, he prowled back into place above her. His glowing amber eyes held her gaze as he lowered himself and pushed inside, filling her in a long, heavy thrust.

And then they were moving together, giving and taking, bodies slick and urgent and driven with a combined need neither of them could deny. It was as if she'd been waiting for this all her long life. Waiting for this man to awaken her and make her feel truly alive.

Sia cried out as wave after wave of release poured over her.

But the pleasure she felt was only the beginning of something larger yet to come. Trygg took her there before she'd barely caught her breath from the first orgasm. She'd never felt such intense desire, and she was no delicate virgin getting a taste of her first lover.

No, this passion she felt with Trygg was unexpected. If she had known it would be this good, she might have leashed the urge to kiss him. Because now, as she looked into his blazing eyes while he chased his own release, all she craved was more.

More from a Breed male who had already pledged himself to another: the Order.

Of all the ways he should be able to terrify her, that thought worried her the most.

Pushing Trygg to kiss her tonight had been an impulse she couldn't control. Now she feared it was a mistake she couldn't undo even if she wanted to. Not that she actually had the will to try. Not when his body was still moving inside her, coaxing her to forget everything except how good they felt together.

Sia groaned, unsure if it was pleasure or misery that pulled the anguished sound from her breast.

Maybe she truly had lost her mind tonight.

All she knew was that if she wasn't careful around him, she might also lose her heart.

Chapter 8

Trygg could have stayed buried inside Sia's soft, wet warmth all night.

He'd lost count of how many times he made her come. His own performance had been one for the records. Hours later, somewhere between midnight and daybreak, she had fallen asleep in his arms. His eyes remained open. Sleep was the last of his concerns. He had a handful of evidence lying on the dresser just out of his reach—evidence that might lead him to Santino—yet he'd just shirked his duty in order to steal a few hours of pleasure with Sia.

No doubt about it, making love to her was worth every second and then some.

Yet when he considered what he'd just done, guilt raked him.

Anger, too—directed only at himself.

He knew better than to let anything distract him from a goal.

Santino might already be regrouping after the bungling of his men's handling of Rosa. If he had moles inside JUSTIS, he might already be aware that the evidence collected from the dead woman's room had gone missing sometime during the night.

And all the while, Trygg had been lost in a blinding, unquenchable need for the woman still dozing at his side.

Damn it.

This could not happen again. He couldn't allow it. Not until he saw this mission through to the end. Then, maybe he could think about Tamisia the Atlantean.

Right now, she was a distraction he could not afford.

Rolling away from her, he moved carefully out of the narrow bed and got dressed.

Rosa's phone and the other items he had retrieved went silently into the pocket of his leather jacket.

He glanced over his shoulder at Sia, indulging in one last look at her beautiful face resting on the pillow. The pale blonde hair that had felt like silk between his fingers was fanned out around her in sexy disarray. The mouth that had given, and taken, such erotic pleasure was softly parted, her lips the same petal pink as her nipples, which tempted him even from across the room.

He wanted to reassure himself that all they had was sex and some unexpected synergy, but even he knew that for a lie. Sia was different than any woman he'd known before, and not only because of what she was. Being Atlantean was the least remarkable thing about her.

Christ. He was too far gone and he'd only had a single night with her.

How useless would he be if he let this thing between them become something more?

What if he actually allowed himself to fall in love with her?

He chopped that idea off at the knees.

There was no room in his life for that kind of weakness. Love was treacherous. It was as cruel a master as the one he'd spent the first part of his life enslaved to…and the one he so stupidly trusted immediately after breaking free from Dragos.

He swore he'd never put himself in those shackles ever again.

And as tempting as Sia was, the only master he served now was his commitment to the Order.

He started to walk away, but a jab of regret slowed him before he took the first step.

Didn't he owe her something at least?

An apology, if nothing else.

Hastily grabbing a pen from a tray on top of the dresser, he took the empty evidence envelope and scrawled a few feeble words on the back of it.

Then he slipped out the door on stealthy assassin's feet.

* * * *

Sia woke up to an empty bed and bright morning sunlight streaming in through the small window of her attic apartment.

Like the tendrils of an amazing dream, Trygg's dark, spicy scent still clung to the thin sheets and her naked skin. But her dark, incredibly passionate lover was gone.

Of course he was. Daylight and the Breed didn't mix.

Still, disappointment made her groan as she threw off the coverlet and drew in a deep breath. She wasn't one to sulk, but the fact that he hadn't woken her before he left drew her mouth into a small pout. Then again, had he roused her to say good-bye, she might have persuaded him to do even more.

No doubt about that, she thought, shivering at the delicious memory of everything they'd done last night.

How long would she have to wait before she saw him again?

Would he call or come back to the shelter tonight? She wasn't the sort of woman to wait for something she wanted, but she didn't even have a way to reach him, short of showing up unannounced at the Order's command center in the heart of the city.

She didn't know what to do with the giddy energy that was zinging through her. It was as foreign as the low thrum of need that was still resonating inside her, making her stomach flutter and flip. That sensation only intensified when she saw the evidence envelope lying on her dresser, a short note written in bold black handwriting across the back of it.

Trygg's handwriting.

She raced over and picked up the message, hardly able to contain her smile.

As soon as she read the first line, all of her excitement drained into the floor.

Sia,

Tonight was great. But it shouldn't have happened. I'm sorry to leave like this. Should have gone before things went too far.

T.

She stared at his hasty scrawl, her face burning as if she'd been slapped. Humiliation swamped her, along with a pain she didn't know what to call.

Of course, she shouldn't be surprised Trygg had left. She was always the one being left or betrayed.

Elyon had used her body for his own amusement and her position on the council to further his deranged political ambitions. Before him, it had been Zael, an Atlantean charmer who had romanced her into his bed whenever the whim struck him, only to leave the colony later and give his heart to a woman who was Breed.

There had been several men who came and went from Sia's immortal past, but, incredibly, Trygg's abrupt rejection stung her the most.

At least he'd been upfront about it.

And she had no one to blame for this morning-after dose of harsh reality except herself.

After all, she'd been the one pushing him.

Hadn't she feared that was a mistake even last night, as she was blissfully, blindly entangled in his arms?

Now she felt so stupid. So miserably embarrassed.

The only saving grace was the fact that she probably would never see Trygg again. He'd make sure of that, she had no doubt.

She could only hope she'd be spared the further mortification of having to face him after practically throwing herself in his lap.

Sia let out a huffed sigh as she tore his message into confetti and dropped it in the trash. All she wanted to do was crawl back into the lumpy bed and pretend this had never happened.

But first she needed a long, hot bath to wash the memory of him from her skin, if not her humiliated conscience.

Donning a robe, she padded out of her small quarters and downstairs to one of the shared bathrooms on the second floor.

Phaedra was just coming out of Rosa's room, a basket of little Angelina's baby clothes and crib toys under her arm. She smiled at Sia. "I suppose we're going to have to empty out this bedroom and make room for another girl before long."

Sia nodded. "I can do it if you like. I'll start right after I finish with my bath."

Phaedra lifted a brow, her tone confidential, even conspiratorial. "I heard a man's voice upstairs last night. I didn't realize you were home and I almost knocked on your door before I realized you were in there with a…guest. Is he still here?"

"No. He's gone. And he won't be back, either. I'm sorry if I worried you." Sia glanced at the items her friend carried, eager to change the subject. "How's Angelina doing?"

"She's a sweet baby. But I know she must miss her mama, even though she won't understand what happened to her for a very long time. The poor thing slept in fits and starts all night. I think it will help to have her crib and some of her toys and other things."

"Of course," Sia agreed. She spotted a bit of soft pink fluff hiding in the midst of the collection Phaedra carried. "No wonder she's having trouble sleeping. She doesn't have her favorite blanket—"

All of a sudden, a prickle of instinct raced through Sia.

She pulled the pink blanket from the basket and held it out before her, searching for something she couldn't name, yet was certain was there.

"What's wrong?" Phaedra asked.

Sia couldn't answer. She zeroed in on the satin binding that ran along the edges of the tiny coverlet. And then she saw what she was looking for—a row of stitches that didn't quite match the rest of them. One small section of the blanket's binding had been loosened then mended.

And something minuscule was sewn inside it.

"Ah, there you are," she whispered as she glanced up at Phaedra, her heart racing with excitement. "Rosa came here because the man she had been involved with—Angelina's father—had run afoul of a very dangerous man. He was killed for something he had on this bad man, and her attackers the other night felt certain that whatever it was, Rosa was in possession of it. They didn't even glance at Angelina when they were in the room and she was wailing and crying. Not even a single look."

Phaedra frowned. "I don't understand."

"This blanket. It was a gift from Angelina's father not long after he told Rosa he was in some kind of trouble." Sia slid her fingernail under the mismatched stitches and started ripping them open. "The men who showed up here looking for Rosa? They were totally focused on her. They dumped her purse and backpack, they rifled through her closet. But what neither of them thought to do was search the crib. Seems like the perfect place to hide something you didn't want someone to find would be—"

"On the baby," Phaedra whispered.

Sia fished inside the hole she'd made and tugged out the tiny item concealed inside.

"It's an SD card," Phaedra said, staring at the fingertip-sized wafer of plastic and circuitry in Sia's palm. "They're used for storing large amounts of data. Tamisia, what do you think is on that card?"

"I don't know. But I know someone who will."

Chapter 9

Trygg swung a battle-ax one-handed, burying the blade all the way into the thick pillar of oak in the training area of the weapons room at the command center. The wood splintered on impact, exploding a hail of jagged shards in all directions.

"Motherfu—" His comrade, Savage, came up from the sudden crouch Trygg's strike had sent him into, his eyes wide beneath his mane of wavy blond hair. He swiveled his head to look at the blow that narrowly missed him, then chuckled. "You asked me to spar with you, asshole, not volunteer as guillotine fodder."

"Just trying to keep your questionable skills sharp," Trygg replied. "You've been spending so much time with that new mate of yours, it'd be a shame to watch you go soft."

Savage smirked. "Being with Arabella does anything but make me go soft. And since when have you given a shit about time I spend with her? Not getting jealous, are you?"

Rather than dignify the jab with an answer, Trygg snarled and brought the ax around for a second swing. Savage spun to dodge it, bringing his own weapon down and driving the iron blade of Trygg's ax into the concrete floor.

"Now who's the one going soft?" Savage taunted with a quick grin.

"Again." Trygg raised his weapon for another round, but Savage held his hands up in surrender.

"Forget it. You've already shaved a couple of inches off my hair with that thing today and Bella needs something to hold on to." When Trygg only grunted in response, his friend cocked his head at him in question. "Something wrong? If I didn't know you better, I'd think you were the one with troubles of the female sort. And since the only woman I ever saw you look twice at was that Atlantean icicle Tamisia a few weeks ago—"

"You know nothing," Trygg grumbled. He relaxed his stance, then strode across the room to stow his weapon in the rack.

"She's still in Rome, you know."

"I am aware."

"Yeah?" Savage came over and racked his weapon too. The warrior stared, then positioned himself so that he was leaning against the wall and watching Trygg's gaze. "Are you also aware that she's here right now?"

"Here?" Trygg replied, hoping he misunderstood.

Savage nodded, looking far too intrigued. "I saw her in Lazaro's office on my way down to spar with you."

Shit. That was nearly an hour ago. "What the hell is Sia doing meeting with the commander?"

Savage arched a brow. "So, she's Sia now, eh? Maybe the Atlantean icicle isn't as chilly as we all thought."

The warrior's obvious amusement with the whole idea made Trygg want to wipe Savage's smile away with another hard bout of combat practice. But he had bigger problems to contend with if Sia had taken it upon herself to contact Lazaro Archer. Especially after last night's fiasco at her apartment.

What was she doing, lodging a formal complaint?

Trygg didn't have to answer to his commander or his warrior brethren about who he chose to get naked with, but knowing that Sia was in the building had him stalking out of the weapons room at a swift clip. Savage strolled along at his heels.

Just as the warrior had claimed, Sia had been in a closed door meeting with Lazaro. The pair were exiting the room together when Trygg approached from the other end of the corridor.

"Ah, there he is now," Lazaro said with a nod. "Trygg, I was just coming to find you."

He couldn't keep from glancing at Sia as the commander spoke. She looked even more beautiful, if that was possible. But while the expression on her face was indifferent, her blue eyes were glacial.

Lazaro gestured to her. "You remember Tamisia."

It wasn't a question. The commander had been informed about the attack on the woman at Sia's shelter, and he was too observant to pretend he wasn't at least peripherally aware of the awkward tension radiating off Trygg and the Atlantean as they faced each other now.

"Tamisia," Trygg said, giving her a nod of greeting while trying to tune out Savage's low snort behind him. Sia's withering gaze was the harder response to ignore. He cleared his throat. "What's going on, Lazaro?"

"This." The commander held a tiny SD card between his fingers. "Thanks to Tamisia's help, we may be back in the game on our hunt for Santino."

"Holy shit." Trygg took the card.

"It's encrypted," Lazaro said, "which only confirms to me that we've got something big here."

Trygg swung his incredulous gaze to Sia. "Where did you get it?"

"Angelina's baby blanket," she answered flatly. "I found it sewn into the binding."

"The one that was a gift from her father, Gianni Tiaggi?"

She gave him a grudging nod.

"Fuck. Of course, it was hidden in the blanket."

Why hadn't he thought of that last night? Because he was too busy thinking about getting Sia naked, that's why. The fact that he was still reliving their time together now just served to fortify his decision to nip their attraction in the bud.

He shook his head as he considered the data card in his palm. "Tiaggi must've figured anyone going after information he might've passed along would never think to search the infant."

Sia shrugged. "Or he didn't care one way or the other. Who can say when it comes to how men think?"

The barb sliced into him, as intended. If her cool demeanor left any question, her flinty tone did not. Sia was pissed as hell. And there was an odd resignation in her eyes when she looked at him. As if she had already written him off and left last night behind in her mind.

And in her heart.

"Do you think you can crack her, Trygg?"

Lazaro's question jolted him for a moment before he realized he was talking about the SD card. "You know I can."

Lazaro nodded. "Then let's go see what's hiding on that card."

* * * *

Lazaro Archer led the way up the corridor, with Savage walking alongside him. To Sia's dismay, Trygg lagged behind his comrades, slowing his long-legged strides to match her pace. The last thing she wanted to do was speak to him, but he seemed determined to have a few words.

"Are you going to tell me the real reason you're here?"

"Isn't it obvious?" She kept walking, refusing to so much as glance at him. "The Order is looking for intel on Roberto Santino and it appears I may have found some."

"You know what I'm asking, Sia." He narrowed a look on her, keeping his deep voice at a tight whisper. "Why bring the evidence to Lazaro instead of coming to me?"

"Oh, was that an option? I'm sorry, I guess I wasn't sure based on the note you left before you slunk out the door while I slept."

"You're upset with me."

"Not at all. You behaved exactly as I should have expected."

He uttered a curse under his breath, then slowed her to a halt with his hand on her wrist. "I said I was sorry about last night."

"Yes, you did." She wrenched free of his loose grasp. "And so am I."

She quickened her pace until she had caught up to his commander and colleague. She felt the heat of Trygg's eyes at her back as she sailed through the door Lazaro held open for her, and into a room filled with computers and other technology.

Trygg entered a moment behind her, stalking over to take the empty seat in front of a bank of monitors and lighted processors.

He said nothing, getting right to work on the data storage card. Sia stood beside Lazaro as Trygg inserted the card into a computer and his fingers flew with speed and grace over the keyboard. She looked on, captivated as he worked.

It seemed odd to watch him excel at this skill, knowing he'd been born and bred to be a killer.

Although no more odd than it felt knowing those same deft, deadly hands had also delivered such intense pleasure last night.

She mentally barred the memory of their lovemaking from her mind. She was here because she wanted the Order to succeed in stopping Santino.

After her conversation with Lazaro Archer today, that mission was all that mattered.

She swallowed hard and watched along with Trygg's comrades as he clicked on the tiny drive's link to open its contents. As Lazaro had discovered when he attempted to open the card's data, the files were protected by an encryption code.

It took Trygg all of three seconds to hack through it.

On the screen, a list of six files labeled with numbers only stared back at them. Trygg opened the first one. It was a text file with what appeared to be a copy-and-paste collection of emails. Each had little content, each dated within the past three weeks, all of them from someone with the user name "il_re."

"The king," Lazaro murmured, his tone sardonic.

Sia's eyes went wide. "Are you saying these are Santino's personal emails?"

"Looks like it." Savage smirked. "*Il Re*. Subtle, the asshole is not."

Trygg opened each file, and Sia excitedly started reading them out loud, translating as she went. "Marina di Ardea still too hot. Scouting new location. Await word before proceeding."

She watched as he scrolled down to the next one, and then the next, her pulse beating faster as she realized they were almost certainly looking at correspondence from Santino to one or more of his lieutenants down the line.

When they reached the end of the list, Lazaro stood back with a frown. "This is a good find, but I have to admit I was hoping for a lot more."

Sia glanced at him. "It may seem insignificant to us, but the contents on this card were enough to cause Gianni Tiaggi to fear for his life—and with good cause, considering his body was found in the river less than a week ago. Whatever information is here was enough for Santino's men to kill Rosa just because they thought she might have it."

"Sia's right," Trygg said. "And the emails aren't the real piece of intel on this."

"Then what is?" Lazaro asked.

Trygg didn't answer. He was completely engrossed in his work now, his dark eyes laser-focused on the screen as he tapped out a few more commands. "There's a hidden file here. I can feel it."

"You can *feel* it?" Sia stared at the side of his rugged face, his scar gleaming in the light of the display. "What is that, a Breed thing?"

He gave her an askance look. "It's my thing."

"We've all got our unique talents," Savage interjected. "My man

Trygg here has a special connection to technological devices. If he can't romance them with his fingers on the keyboard, he can undress them with his mind. Kind of makes up for his lack of finesse when it comes to people."

Savage winked at her as he said it, which made Sia's face flush with a fresh wave of embarrassment. Had Trygg told his friend about what they'd done last night? She lifted her chin as if she didn't care one way or the other, but inside she was dying.

"What kind of hidden file do you think we've got here?" Lazaro asked, leaning one hand on the desk beside Trygg to have a closer look.

"Not sure yet," he murmured. "Probably something Tiaggi didn't want Santino to know he had even if someone did find the card. But I've got a way around that."

Trygg accessed a program that split the screen. On one side was the list of six files. On the other was a working string of code that seemed to be connecting to the data on the card, searching for fissures in the encryption. Finally a window popped up, but instead of opening, it displayed a denied access error and password prompt.

"Another firewall," Sia muttered, losing patience. It wasn't only that she wanted the data as badly as any of the warriors in the room with her, it was the fact that being this close to Trygg was wreaking havoc on her senses. Her frustration came out of her in an exhaled huff. "I thought you said you could crack it."

"I have." He stopped tapping on the keyboard and closed his eyes for a moment, his face held in utter concentration. A moment later, the window disappeared and a file opened. Strings of multi-digit numbers filled the screen.

Sia peered at them, trying to find some logic in the sequences. "What are those?"

Trygg gave her a grim smile as they kept scrolling, page after page after page. "I'm guessing by the looks of them, it's a list of Swiss bank accounts."

"Holy shit," Savage hissed. "If that's true, we could be looking at potentially accessing billions of dollars' worth of Santino's assets. If we play our cards right, we could have his accounts drained in hours."

"True," Lazaro said. "And that is good news. But a broke Santino isn't nearly as good as a dead Santino."

Trygg was still skimming the list when he paused his cursor over one set of numbers with degree marks beside them.

"What's wrong?" Sia asked, leaning in to read them.

"This set of numbers is different. They aren't account numbers. They're coordinates, followed by what looks like a date and a time."

He opened a new window and typed one set of coordinates into a search engine. A second later, a map of southern Italy filled the screen with a pin right over the Sicilian port city of Trapani.

"These are delivery schedules," he murmured.

"Two nights from now," she replied breathlessly, catching on to the number sequence and seeing the date now, her body humming with energy and adrenaline. They were so close to being able to take that bastard down now, she could taste it.

Savage grinned. "Whatever Santino is up to with these messages, looks like it's going to happen in Trapani."

Lazaro clapped Trygg on the shoulder. "Knew I could count on you. I need to call Lucan and let him know what we've uncovered."

The commander walked into the hallway, his phone already held at his ear. Savage left the room without any excuse at all, leaving Sia and Trygg alone once more.

"Admit it," he said after a moment, swiveling around in his chair. "You're impressed."

She scoffed. "Just because you have some obvious skill with the rather rudimentary technology of this world? Hardly."

He shrugged. "Well, you impress me, Sia. Looking for the data card in the baby blanket was... That was really smart. We'd have nothing right now if you hadn't put that together. Thank you."

She hadn't expected his praise, nor his gratitude. The fact that he offered it left her confused and unsteady. She'd come here fueled on anger and a bruised sense of pride. More than that, she'd gone to Lazaro Archer with a bitter, wounded heart. Now, Trygg was acting as if they were still a team—albeit an unwilling one.

She couldn't let herself fall for it so easily. Hadn't she learned a thing after Elyon and the other men who had walked all over her to get what they wanted?

Now, it was her turn to win something just for her. Something she wanted.

And she had every intention of doing just that.

"I've asked Lazaro to let me assist in the mission to take down Santino."

Trygg shot out of his chair, his dark brows crashing together. "You what?"

"I asked him, and he agreed."

He gaped at her as if she'd just sprouted a horn in the middle of her forehead. "Why the fuck would he agree to that?"

Lazaro's deep voice provided the answer. "Because Tamisia has already proven herself an asset to us on this operation. Without her, we'd still be chasing our tails looking for the slimmest threads to lead us to the son of a bitch. Now, we've got emails, account numbers, and a possible jump on Santino's distribution schedules."

Trygg looked positively furious. "I don't like it. This is my mission, Lazaro. I don't want a female standing in the way—"

Sia gasped. "Standing in the way? You just said yourself that I impressed you. You said I was smart—"

"Yes, you are," Trygg interrupted. "So be smart, Sia. Let the Order handle this. We don't need to be worried about you getting hurt."

She glared at him. "I can take care of myself. I think I've already demonstrated that to you more than once." Heat tingled in her palms. She didn't have to glance at them to know they were filling with energy. "I'm not a weak little woman that you have to look out for, warrior. I could put you on your ass right now. I am your equal, Trygg."

"I never said you weren't."

Lazaro's gaze pivoted between them. "Good. Then that's settled. Trygg, meet your new partner. I've already decided. She's in. And frankly, we need her. Lucan just informed me that they're hearing talk that Santino's cousin, Marco Crespo, has returned to Italy."

Trygg grunted. "I thought that dumbfuck moved permanently to the States six months ago."

"Well, now he's back for some reason. We need to find out why." Lazaro looked at Sia. "That's where you come in."

Sia caught Trygg's disapproving glare, but she tuned him out and smiled at his commander. "Tell me what I need to do."

Chapter 10

It was a crisp night with a fat, full moon hanging in the inky sky. The kind of night that seemed to be begging for trouble, but Trygg shook off the sense of unrest as he sat behind the wheel of a nondescript sedan, counting down the minutes before he could enter the busy club a block up the street.

Tonight's operation was already in motion, with Sia somewhere inside the building acting as bait to get close to Marco Crespo.

Trygg didn't like it.

In fact, he fucking hated the idea of the Order using her for any reason. But she had other ideas—other plans of some kind, he suspected—and there would have been no talking her out of this assignment regardless of what he wanted. She'd made that perfectly clear. And he had no claim on her, so what the hell.

This was going to go nice and smooth, and then he would be flying solo again.

Still, he let out a low growl as he killed the engine and stepped out onto the pavement.

As they'd arranged, Sia had arrived ten minutes before he rolled up. If she was following the plan, she should be inside the club making sure Crespo noticed her. They wanted their mark to be thoroughly engrossed in a potential new conquest so he would be less likely to notice the hulking Breed male from the Order lurking in the shadows, making sure nothing went wrong.

Trygg crossed the parking area in long, unhurried strides, taking stock of the other vehicles in the lot. He smirked as he passed the poison-green Ferrari belonging to Crespo. Santino's cousin had slanted the vehicle across two parking spaces just in case anyone didn't realize he was an asshole when they got a look at his toupee.

Crespo had a reputation as a basic slimeball, but he was also a shallow pool when it came to intellect—all good news as far as tonight's op was concerned.

The rest of Santino's inner circle were so careful, so well-trained, they rarely slipped up. But Crespo had a weakness for beautiful women, and that's where Sia came in. All she had to do was get close enough to put a tracker on him without detection.

As paranoid as Santino was, just bugging the cars wouldn't be enough. But tonight Trygg had something different for them. A new, microscopic bug he had created that clung to the skin like an undetectable burr and melded even more tightly when wet. The connection only lasted a week or so, but that was more than enough time to get what they needed.

Buoyed by the thought, Trygg reached the door to the club and went inside. Almost instantly, he was swamped with the smell of junkies, human and Breed alike. He stifled a cough as he breathed it all in. Heroin, crack, even Red Dragon.

All vile stuff, but it was the Dragon that turned his stomach most.

If any of the Breed males inside the club were high on that shit and decided they wanted a taste of Sia…

His fists clenched at his sides at the very idea. As crucial as this mission was, he'd cut a bloody swath through the whole damn place if it meant keeping her safe. Whether or not she needed—or wanted—his help.

He made his way toward a corner booth, determined to garner as little notice as possible. A waitress swooped in on him almost immediately. He placed an order just as an attempt to blend in, but all of his attention was focused on the other side of the crowded room.

Sia was impossible to miss, seated at a high table near the bar.

He hadn't seen her arrive, so the sight of her dressed in a skintight black mini-dress that plunged low in front and down to the base of her spine hit him like a shotgun blast. High-heeled ebony boots completed the look, rising up over her knees.

Holy. Fuck.

To say she was hot was the understatement of the century.

Her hair was pulled back into a high ponytail that should have looked severe but only managed to make her face look that much more striking. Tonight those wide-set, sky-blue eyes were highlighted with shadow and kohl liner, the effect making them take up the majority of her preternaturally perfect face. Her lush lips were slicked with deep plum gloss and her already iridescent skin was dusted with something that made it glimmer like diamonds under the colored strobes as she threw her head back and laughed at something Marco Crespo whispered in her ear.

The bastard would've had to be blind, deaf, *and* dumb not to notice her.

Hell, she was having an obvious effect on every man in the club.

And Trygg was no exception.

As his drink arrived, part of him wanted to laugh at how easily she had reeled Crespo in. But the rest of him wanted to flip the fucking table over, march toward her, and drag her out of this place before Crespo or any other male decided to put their hands on her.

Too late for that.

His vision took on an amber haze as he idly held his beer bottle and watched Crespo's arm go around her bare back. Trygg caught her subtle flinch, but only because he knew her lovely body so well. Crespo was too dense to notice her revulsion, and she was careful to cover it up with a saucy smile and a playful bat of her long lashes.

Trygg's blood boiled.

How long would he have to endure this irritating act?

He had hardly completed the thought when Crespo stood suddenly, tugged a few bills from his pocket, and tossed them onto the bar. He gestured to the pack of four thugs who'd evidently accompanied him to stay behind, then he held out his hand and Sia took it, allowing him to draw her to her feet. The motion put them face to face, her mouth only inches from Crespo's. A hot rage like Trygg had never felt rolled through his chest as his fangs punched through his gums.

No fucking way was he letting her walk out of here with that piece of shit. Letting Santino's cousin take her out of the club was not part of the fucking deal.

But Sia was the one leading the way, shooting a coy glance over her shoulder at Crespo as she led him toward the back exit.

They disappeared and the sound of glass cracking jarred Trygg out of his rage. He glanced down to find his fist wrapped around a shattered brown bottle, blood and beer leaking all over the lacquered tabletop.

"Fuck this." He swung out of the booth on a snarl.

Rather than stalk past Crespo's companions, he slipped out the front of the club and rounded the building in a flash of motion. It took him a moment to find Sia. She was hidden in the shadows at the back of the parking lot, Marco Crespo's hands roaming all over her like an octopus.

Every muscle in Trygg's body vibrated with unleashed fury.

Sia must have caught the glow of his eyes in the dark. She shook her head at him as if she had it under control, but Trygg was already in motion.

"Get your fucking hands off her." His deep snarl rent the night air.

He knew he was interfering with the operation, but damn it, he couldn't help it. He didn't care how capable Sia was of handling herself. He didn't care how crucial this mission was, either. If the Order needed a female to act as bait for Santino or any of the scum who served him, they'd have to volunteer one of their own women.

Not his.

"I said hands off, asshole. Right. Fucking. Now."

"Huh?" Crespo staggered around to look at him, his face twisted with confusion and anger at the intrusion. He took one look at Trygg, then glanced at Sia, his expression murderous. "You set me up, bitch?"

She stared at him coldly and took a step away.

But just as his reputation might have predicted, Santino's dim cousin did the stupidest thing he possibly could. Pulling a gun from inside his jacket, he raised it in front of Sia's forehead.

Hell, no.

Trygg pounced before he even realized his body was in motion. Leaping the distance between him and Crespo, he took the human down like a bear on a field mouse.

"Trygg, don't!"

Sia's panicked shout barely registered through the blinding red of his rage. He heard a gunshot crack louder than thunder as Crespo's weapon fired a wild shot on his descent to the pavement, but not even that made a dent in his fury.

Trygg wrenched the human's head so violently it was a miracle it didn't separate from Crespo's shoulders. He roared like an animal, barely leashing the urge to rip the corpse to pieces just for the offense of touching Sia.

But then Trygg caught a whiff of fresh-spilled blood somewhere nearby.

Sia. She was on the ground, her long legs gone out from under her when the bullet tore into her right thigh.

Son of a bitch. She'd been hit.

He knew she would heal on her own, but seeing her bloodied and down on the ground made his veins freeze.

And then they were no longer alone.

The club's rear door banged open several yards behind them, bringing the pounding beat from inside and the chatter of anxious male voices with it.

"Marco said to stay put," one of the humans whined. "He's not going to be happy if we interrupt him."

Another man answered. "He's gonna be a lot less happy if that Breed male I spotted came out here to try and steal that hot blonde tail he's trying to lock up tonight."

"I'm telling you, that vampire is from the Order," a third male voice interjected grimly. "I think he's that Gen One from the Rome unit."

Someone else chuckled. "Better hope he's not, or Marco and all the rest of us are—"

"Fucked," Trygg answered, stepping into the light.

The men stopped abruptly and a lot of weapons were drawn. Trygg wasn't sure who fired first. All he knew was that after a brief, chaotic hail of gunshots and pained cries, Roberto Santino was minus one dumbfuck cousin and four of his foot soldiers.

"I can't believe you did this." Sia came up next to him, already walking on her own. The look she swiveled on him was bleak, something more than incredulous. "You killed them all."

"Yes." He turned to her, sliding the hot barrel of his 9-millimeter into the back waistband of his black jeans. "Are you okay?"

In the end, that was the only thing that mattered. She didn't answer right away, but he could see that her Atlantean skin was mending as he watched. The sweet honey-and-citrus scent of her blood still clung to her, making his senses throb and his fangs stretch even longer behind his curled upper lip.

He reached out to touch her, if only to reassure himself that she was fine. She flinched away from his touch.

"No one was supposed to die," she murmured woodenly. "Those were our orders, Trygg. Plant the bug on Crespo and get out. That's what Lazaro expected us to do."

He shook his head on a curse. "I don't give a shit about that right now."

"Well, I do!" She shoved at him and started marching away from the carnage.

He caught up in a blink, blocking her path. "What the hell are you so upset about? I did this because of you. Don't you understand that? When Crespo pulled that gun on you, I thought—"

"You thought what?" she shot back. "That you needed to protect me? I didn't ask you to. Dammit, Trygg, I don't want your protection. All I want is—"

She cut herself off on a miserable-sounding groan.

"All you want is what?" he demanded. "Say it, Sia. For fuck's sake, tell me what this is about."

Her gaze was stark, even accusing. "All I want is a chance to get back home to the colony. To my people. Back where I belong."

He drew back. He hadn't been expecting that. She had admitted to him once before that a day didn't pass when she hadn't thought of her old life. He just hadn't considered how deeply she obviously wanted it. Especially since she'd been banished from ever returning.

And that raised a question that had been troubling him ever since he'd seen her at the command center earlier today.

"What does this mission have to do with your getting back to the colony?"

Her bleak look said it all. "I made a deal with Lazaro Archer. I'll assist the Order in any way I can to help get rid of Santino, and he'll do whatever he can to convince my people to allow me to return home."

The truth of her words belted him like a punch but he kept his face impassive. "That's a long shot and you know it."

"Yes, I know that. But it was the only hope I had." She glanced past him to the dead bodies and the end of yet another lead on Santino. "You just took that hope away from me."

Trygg tried to harden himself to the sadness in her eyes, the desperation. But it wasn't easy to do. Not when the one thing he wanted was for her to stay. Not just in Rome, but with him. He should have told her that before now.

His chest felt hollow in the silence that stretched out between them. He ached with an emotion he could neither name nor reconcile.

He felt bereft as he watched her pivot on her sky-high heels and start marching away from him. He felt strangely empty and alone.

Fuck no.

This wouldn't do. This hurt, this yearning.

This weakness where she was concerned.

He should be glad for her animosity toward him. He should be eager for the chance to see her gone from his city and his life.

He told himself he was.

He promised himself that since what Sia wanted most was to be rid of him and be free to go back to her own kind, he would do everything in his power to make that happen.

Chapter 11

"I thought I'd find you up here," Phaedra said the next morning, joining Sia on the roof of the shelter house.

Her Atlantean friend had fashioned one area of the rooftop into a private garden space filled with large potted plants, blooming flower beds, citrus trees, and marble statuary. It was small, just five hundred square feet of tranquility, but it was a tiny slice of paradise, the closest thing to home that Sia had found anywhere else in the city.

She soaked in the peace and quiet, her arms spread out at her sides, her head tipped back to greet the newly risen sun. The cleansing rays poured into her, soothing and warm. This was a ritual for their kind, one required to rejuvenate both their bodies and souls.

Today, Sia needed healing on every level possible, most especially her heart.

Phaedra offered a concerned smile. "How are you holding up?"

"I'm fine. Much better today." It was mostly a lie, but she was tired of feeling sorry for herself. She had plenty of time for that when she was alone. "It's beautiful up here."

Phaedra inclined her head at the praise. "This is the only space in the house that's off-limits for the other residents. Sometimes I feel guilty for not sharing it."

Sia smiled. "Thank you for sharing it with me."

"The pleasure is mine, Tamisia. I have enjoyed having you here." She quieted, growing reflective. "I only wish you were happier on this side of the veil, my dear friend."

"I suppose I'll have to learn to be, right?"

Phaedra nodded gently, aware of Sia's wish to go home and her dashed hopes after last night. When she'd returned to the house with blood on her dress and the acrid stench of bar odors and gun smoke in her hair, Sia'd had little choice but to explain what happened—and why.

She didn't have to confess about her feelings for Trygg, but she'd been an emotional wreck and it had helped having someone to lean on. Phaedra had listened patiently, offering no judgment for Sia's foolishness in getting involved with a man who was incapable of seeing her as anything other than an obligation, a liability.

But it was worse than that. Sia had allowed herself to care for Trygg the way she never had for any other man.

When she wasn't frustrated or infuriated with him, she was terrified of having to admit to the realization she might actually be falling in love with him.

Which only made the prospect of remaining in Rome even less appealing.

"Maybe I should travel the globe," she mused aloud, resuming her meditation. With her eyes closed and her face tipped back into the sun, she tried to imagine all of the wondrous places she could explore in this mortal world. "I could go wherever my whim takes me, then pick up and move on to the next adventure before I even have a chance to get bored. If I want to, I could take a new lover in every port—or two!"

Phaedra laughed beside her. "It sounds exciting."

Sia nodded, but behind her closed eyelids she felt nothing. She might enjoy seeing new places and doing new things, but the most engaged she'd felt in a very long time was right here, working at the shelter.

And then she'd crossed paths with Trygg. He'd made her feel alive. He'd made her crave, for the first time ever, a life outside of the colony. A life with him. At his side, as his partner in more than just his missions with the Order.

But that's not how he saw her.

He proved that last night when he'd yanked certain victory out of her hands because he didn't trust her to see it through without his interference.

She'd wasted enough of her days—and her nights—being pushed around and underestimated by men. Perhaps it was unfair to put Trygg in that category so soon, but she'd meant it when she told him she could protect herself just fine on her own.

And right now, the smartest thing she could do was protect herself from the irreversible mistake of falling in love with him.

Which meant putting as much distance as possible between them.

She drifted deep into her own thoughts as she and Phaedra completed the rest of their morning meditation in silence. When they finished, Phaedra turned to her, considering her for a long moment.

"In case you don't know this, Tamisia, you deserve happiness. Wherever you decide to look for it."

Sia shook her head. "No, I probably don't—"

"Yes, you do." Phaedra unfastened the leather thong attached to her wrist. The small silvery orb of Atlantean crystal sparkled as she freed the bracelet and held it out to Sia. "I want you to have this."

"No, I cannot." She shook her head. "That crystal is yours."

"I don't need it anymore. I haven't needed this for a very long time. I am exactly where I want to be." She smiled conspiratorially. "Use it to take you on all of your exciting travels."

"Phaedra, no. I didn't actually mean any of that. I was only pretending I wanted to do those things."

"Then use it to take you home," she said, affixing the strip of warm leather to Sia's wrist in spite of her protests. "Plead your own case to the council. If you need someone to vouch for your honor and your worthiness to be accepted back into the colony's fold, I will testify for you. Mine is only one voice, but there was a time when it meant something in the realm. I will help you in any way I can."

Sia glanced back down at her wrist and at the extraordinarily generous gift from her friend. "Phaedra, thank you for this. And for everything else you've given me since I arrived here. Thank you for being my friend."

"The honor is mine." With a placid smile, she rested her hand lightly on Sia's arm. "How about some tea?"

Sia nodded, but she couldn't find her voice. Her throat was tight and her eyes stung as she stared at the glimmering, otherworldly amulet. The magical chunk of cosmic stone would carry her anywhere her heart desired. Even back to the colony.

She only needed to have the will to use it.

Chapter 12

Savage was waiting in the corridor as Trygg came out of a closed-door meeting in Lazaro Archer's office late that afternoon. "How'd it go in there?"

"About as good as you might expect."

Savage grunted. "Shit. That bad, huh?"

"Five dead bodies, and one of them just happens to be an embedded JUSTIS operative who'd been working Santino's crew for the past two months." Trygg shook his head. "The commander should've handed me more than just my ass. If Lucan Thorne had his way, I'd be tossed out on it right now."

Trygg's own honor—thin as it was—practically demanded he resign his post with the Order and find something else to do with his time and varied skills. The fuck-up outside the club with Sia was completely his fault. He'd lost all sense of reason when he watched Crespo leave with her. Seeing the bastard pawing Sia out in the parking lot like some barfly whore had pushed him right to the edge of a red fury he couldn't leash. But it was the scent of her spilled blood—the realization she'd been wounded—that had obliterated all of his logic and control.

He'd not only forfeited the night's mission to track a member of Santino's inner circle, he'd jeopardized months of work for both the Order and a covert team inside JUSTIS.

To put a cherry on top of the whole stinking pile of mistakes, he'd also lost Sia in the process.

They had gone their separate ways after the massacre at the club. She headed straight to the shelter on foot, a fact he knew only because he covertly followed her there, needing to be certain for his own peace of mind that she made it home without issue.

As for him, he'd been at the command center ever since, doing his damnedest to glean more intel off the SD card and any other data lead he could chase down. What he really wanted to do was smash something with his bare fists.

Sia was livid with him and for good reason, evidently.

He still couldn't believe she had planned to return to her colony without so much as telling him about it.

Then again, if she was that hellbent to get back to her people, who was he to stand in her way?

He should be the one holding the damn door open for her to walk her haughty ass out of his life, out of his thoughts. Out of his heart.

Her fine ass, he corrected himself grimly.

But he didn't want to think about that or any other of Sia's many fine qualities.

He had a mission to put back on the rails and he intended to do it.

Savage broke into his thoughts as the two of them started down the corridor. "What do you suppose the odds are that Santino's business in Trapani tonight is still a go?"

Trygg shook his head. "We can't be sure, but we also can't risk losing the chance to find out. Lazaro and Lucan just gave me my orders. I'll be heading south to stake out the area as soon as the sun sets."

Savage cocked his head. "A stakeout? Last I knew, we were gearing up for a raid if the lead turns out to be a hot one."

Trygg swiveled a flat look at him. "Change of plans, courtesy of JUSTIS. Since I put a wrench in their side investigation, they're demanding the Order surrender any collars to them. If there's a bust to be made, they get the win. We've just been downgraded to an eyes and ears operation only."

Savage scoffed. "In other words, we do all the work, and then we phone it in to JUSTIS for them to take the credit?"

"Sounds about right," Trygg muttered. "Lazaro and Lucan aren't happy about it, either, but since we all want Santino put out of the Red Dragon business, we've got to play nice—at least for now. Lucan and the team in D.C. have their own problems with JUSTIS and the layers of corruption that have infected the organization. As for me, I don't give a shit who I report to. I just want to see the job done and Santino wiped off the board for good."

As they approached the residential area of the command center, the sound of female voices carried from one of the rooms on the main floor. To hear Savage's mate, Arabella, and Lazaro's mate, Melena, was no surprise, but it was the other soft voice that made Trygg's feet slow beneath him.

Sia.

Trygg couldn't hide his surprise as he and Savage reached the large arched entryway and found the three women seated together on the sofa and chairs inside. They had a tray of fruits and cheese in front of them and glasses of red wine in their hands.

Trygg's gaze rooted on Sia. "What are you doing here?"

"Nice to see you too." Her tone was cooler than her gaze. In fact, if he knew anything at all about females, he might have guessed she'd been crying recently. "I came to say good-bye to my friends."

"Good-bye?" He tried to ignore the disapproving looks of the two women. "You mean you're leaving Rome?"

She nodded and his heart felt as if it were suddenly caught in a fist. "When?"

"As soon as possible. Tomorrow, most likely."

Fuck. He would be gone to Trapani in a few hours on a mission that would easily last most of the night. Which meant the odds of seeing her again after this moment were slim to none. He told himself it was for the best. If seeing her right now felt like hot iron talons raking deep into his chest, what would he feel like if he had to watch her leave?

"Where are you going to go?" His words came out rough, more demand than question.

"I haven't decided yet. I may eventually go back to the colony and appeal to the council to pardon me."

"I see."

Just then, he noticed the leather thong that looped her wrist, its small crystal orb shimmering in the soft light of the room. He knew what the crystal was. The Atlantean male and friend of the Order's, Zael, wore the same kind of teleportation amulet around his wrist. It was how he transported himself between the mortal world and his own.

Now Sia had one too. From her friend Phaedra at the shelter, if he had to guess.

So, her mind was truly made up. One way or another, Sia was determined to go back where she belonged. He nodded, the tendons in his neck feeling tight.

"Okay. Then good luck to you, Sia."

Before he was tempted to say any of the lame things that were leaping to his tongue, he wheeled around and stalked out of the room without another word.

He got all the way to his quarters and had stormed inside the room when Sia's voice sounded in the open doorway.

"That's it? That's all you're going to say to me?"

He stood in the center of the room, his glower trained on her as he turned to face her. "What do you expect me to say?"

Her answering laugh was brittle. "You're right. This is exactly what I should expect. I'm sorry if I'm bothering you with my presence, Trygg." She turned around, then seemed to reconsider almost as swiftly. "No. You know what? I'm not sorry I'm bothering you. I'm sorry that you weren't like this before."

"Before what, Sia?"

"Before I threw myself at you like a fool the other night. If you'd been this cold and detached all along, none of it would have happened."

He wasn't so certain of that, but he didn't point it out. "Fortunately, once you're gone we won't have even more to regret."

She flinched as if he'd just struck her. "What a cruel thing to say."

"Is it?" He honestly didn't know. A remorseful sigh gusted out of him. "I'm not good at this, Sia. I don't know what things to say that won't hurt you. All I really know how to do is to hunt, to kill. That's who I am."

"No. That's what you were forced to be as a child." She stepped farther inside the room. "Who you are now is up to you. The same way I now need to decide who I am going to be."

"You do know, Sia. That bracelet tells me you've already made your choice."

She touched the crystal orb, then glanced up at him with a plea in her eyes. "Then help me change my mind, Trygg."

He stepped back, possibly the first time he'd ever retreated from anything in his life. "Don't ask me to. I don't have anything to offer you. Not while Santino is alive."

She remained silent for a long moment, emotion playing over her lovely face. When she finally spoke, there was a quiet resignation to her voice. "Then offer me the truth before I go. Why is it so important to you that Roberto Santino is stopped?"

"You know why. I've told you, I've pledged my arm to the Order and this is a mission I intend to see through to the end."

But Sia was too smart to let it go at that. She listened in silence, but her gaze was anything but satisfied with his rote answer. "Why are you pursuing Santino so single-mindedly, Trygg? Is it to put a stop to the pain he's causing the Breed population with his dealing in Red Dragon, or is it because of how you described the way he's using young boys?"

"Isn't either one of those reasons enough for anyone to want the asshole dead?"

"Yes, it is," she replied quietly. "But I'm asking about you." She took another step toward him. "Can't you at least let me in long enough to tell me what happened to you? Trygg, did Roberto Santino—"

"No. It wasn't him." His answer was sharp and quick, like the slice of a blade. Trygg rubbed the scar that ran the length of his cheek. He had no intention of taking this jaunt down memory lane, least of all with Sia.

But she was pushing him to give her his truth. Pushing him like she had the other night in her apartment. She had been pushing him out of the safety of his darkness and into her light all along.

"I was fourteen when my Hunter's collar came off," he told her, each word a whip as it left his mouth. "The lab where Dragos kept us was suddenly open, the locks undone. My cage and all the other boys' were sprung open. We scattered. We all just…ran. I wandered New England for several months. It was snowing, bitter cold, when a human woman saw me walking barefoot on the side of the highway in Connecticut and pulled over to pick me up. Her name was Vicky. She had yellow hair and a smile that seemed to take up half her face. She offered me shelter and a bed. Her bed. But I didn't know that when I got into her car."

Sia winced as he spoke, tenderness in her eyes.

"She lived in a rundown apartment building in one of the bigger cities. There were always men coming and going, often dozens in a day. Sometimes she sold them drugs. Other times she sold them her body. After a while, she started selling mine. She pimped me out to women, men, multiples. Anyone who would pay."

Sia made a sickened, strangled noise. "You were just a child."

"At fourteen I was hardly a child," he corrected tonelessly. "But I knew nothing about sex or addiction. I didn't know enough about people to realize she was using me."

"She did more than use you, Trygg. What she did was unconscionable."

He shrugged, in no need of sympathy. He knew his gaze was sharp and cutting as he held hers now, but he didn't care. He couldn't allow himself to care what Sia thought of him or he might finally break like he never had before.

"I traded one form of enslavement for another. Dragos kept me prisoner with a UV collar. Vicky chained me with kind words, at least at first. I let her trade me because I thought she cared about me, even loved me. When I finally saw through her lies, I told her I was leaving. To make sure she understood I was serious, I shaved my head to get rid of the long black hair she insisted I keep. She was livid. She came at my face with a kitchen knife."

Sia swallowed, her horrified gaze drifting to his scar. "Oh, Trygg."

He smiled coldly. "I could've stopped her before she cut me. I allowed it to happen. I let her ruin my looks, then I turned the blade on her and slit her throat. I left that same night and never looked back."

Now Sia's horror seemed to tilt on its axis. Good. Better she look at him with wariness, even fear, than let her last moments with him be ones of pity.

Trygg chuckled humorlessly. "I told you what I was, Sia. A killer. Maybe now you understand."

She shook her head. "You defended yourself. But why did you let the wound stay after you left Vicky? You're Breed. Your body should have healed itself before leaving a scar like that."

"I didn't want it to heal. I wanted a reminder, so I starved myself for blood as long as I could afterward. My body was too depleted to mend."

"And you keep your hair shorn as a reminder too," she murmured softly. "Trygg, I'm so sorry. I'm sorry for everything you've had to endure."

He blew out a harsh breath. "Don't be. You asked for answers, and I gave them to you. Now, go back to your perfect, sheltered little world with your people and leave me to my business here."

He turned away from her as a dismissal, waiting to hear her footsteps leaving the room. But she didn't leave. She came up behind him and her hands rested gently on his back.

"What more do you want, Sia?"

"I want you. Don't you see that?" Her cheek was warm where she pressed it against him. "Don't let me walk away like this. I want to feel your arms around me again. I need it, Trygg. Even if it's the last time."

He stiffened, steeling himself to all of the emotions that warred inside him at the thought of her leaving for good. When he pivoted to face her, he knew his eyes were ablaze with amber. "One last fuck before you go, is that it?" His words were cruel, but they were the only defensive weapon he had as he stared into her stricken gaze. "I don't perform on command anymore, Sia. And I don't need your pity."

She staggered back on her heels. Tears welled in her wide blue eyes, but they didn't fall. Her breast was heaving, her mouth slack as she mutely shook her head.

Then she slowly turned away from him and walked out the door.

Chapter 13

Sia felt numb as she left Trygg's quarters.

Her heart broke for the unimaginable pain and abuse he'd described. She ached to comfort him, but he hadn't wanted that. He wanted nothing from her anymore, and his rejection opened up a hollow inside her unlike anything she'd ever known.

All the more reason for her to go and never look back.

But leaving Trygg was the last thing she felt ready to do.

Bella and Melena were waiting in the room when she returned. They took one look at her stricken face and rushed to her, ushering her back inside with tender words of concern.

"What happened? Are you all right?"

"Come in and sit down, Sia. You look as if you're about to collapse."

She felt like she could crumble, and the depth of her sorrow shocked her. "I really should go," she murmured, shaking her head. "You've all been so kind, and I appreciate that more than you can know. But I have things to attend to before I—"

The sound of heavy boot falls pounding in the corridor drew all of the women's attention.

Melena's brows knit in apprehension. "What on earth?"

She and Bella hurried out to the hallway. Sia followed anxiously behind them, just in time to see Trygg jogging past dressed in full combat gear.

"Has something happened?" Bella asked.

He slanted the women a look as he passed, his gaze barely skimming Sia's. "The tracer we put on Santino's email address just spit out an alert. He's got a cargo shipment leaving the port of Naples in two hours, heading for Trapani."

"What happened to reconnaissance?" Melena asked Lazaro as her mate and Savage joined Trygg in the corridor, all of them garbed for combat. "I thought JUSTIS was going to handle the takedown?"

"No time for reconnaissance," Lazaro said. "Lucan wants this handled now. JUSTIS can thank us afterward."

Melena and Bella offered hasty but tender good-byes to their mates, while Sia stood by awkwardly, watching Trygg head out to the waiting vehicle with grim, solitary purpose.

In moments, the team had departed, leaving the women to monitor the mission back at the command center. Sia probably should have taken that as her cue to leave, but nothing could have persuaded her to go when she knew Trygg and his comrades were heading into a potentially lethal confrontation.

She hurried into the war room with the two Breedmates and settled in for what she feared was going to be a long, worrisome night.

* * * *

Just under two hours later, Trygg and his teammates arrived in the crowded, ancient city of Naples. The port was busy with tugboats and container ships loading and unloading in the dark. Impossible to determine which of the half dozen holds might contain Santino's goods.

Trygg and Savage split up to cover more ground on foot, each of them keeping to the shadows as they sniffed around the crates and cartons of incoming and outgoing supplies. Lazaro had set out on his own to see if he might spot Santino or any of his lieutenants lurking around the wharf or in town. If the kingpin's messages were anything to go by, tonight's shipment was a high-value, top-priority one for his organization.

Which almost certainly meant a shitload of Red Dragon.

"Got a lot of movement on the south dock," Savage reported over the receiver in Trygg's ear. "I'm going in for a closer look."

"Copy that," Trygg murmured.

He had his eye on another cargo ship—a smaller one that was calling little attention to itself as its lines were cast off and it moved quietly away from the far end of the moonlit wharf. Whatever this unremarkable ship carried, it was apparently already secured inside.

Trygg's Hunter instincts prickled to attention.

This was Santino's ship, he had no doubt.

Although his orders were to surveil the docks and report to his teammates with any unusual activity, there was no time to waste. If he wanted a look at what that ship carried, he was going to have to get on board.

"I think I found something," he whispered into his comm device. "I'm going in."

Without waiting for a reply, he sped to the end of the dock and leapt off. His Breed agility carried him straight up to the rear deck. He landed soundlessly, dropping into a tight roll that took him behind a large wooden crate.

A group of five crew members in gray coveralls manned the deck. They didn't notice him as he crept along in the dark, making his way to the stairwell that led to the holds below as the ship pushed farther out to sea. He waited a few minutes until the coast was clear, then he ducked inside and headed down the metal steps.

In his ear, Lazaro's deep voice crackled in a broken string of impatient words. "Trygg. DC. Intel. Abort."

Shit. Even garbled and full of static, that didn't sound good.

But Trygg was already in the cargo hold, and he could smell the sickly sweet odor of Red Dragon coming from the cartons stacked row upon row in front of him. He freed the lock on one of the containers and threw off the cables that secured it. Prying open the lid of the large carton, he peered inside. It wasn't what he expected.

Instead of a carton packed to the gills with the Breed-killing narcotic, there were only a few sealed bags inside. Just enough to leave a scent for anyone searching for them. Anyone Breed, that is.

Specifically, someone from the Order.

Jesus Christ.

Trygg reached in and moved some of the bags aside.

The real cargo lay beneath them. Trygg's nostrils filled with the acrid metallic odor of explosives. Enough to take down half a city block.

Or a small cargo ship.

* * * *

"Oh, my God." Melena's face went slack as she ended her call with Lazaro. "It's all been a trap."

Bella gaped. "A trap? What do you mean?"

"They were set up. The intel Trygg's email worm provided was false. Santino only wanted the Order to think he had a shipment of Red Dragon leaving Naples. He was hoping to lure them out to intercept the shipment for some reason."

Bella's gaze was grave. "There's only one reason for him to do that."

Sia saw the worry in her friends' faces and knew her own must look equally stark. "Where's Trygg?"

Melena gave her a sober look. "Lazaro lost contact with him a couple of minutes ago. He's been trying to warn him, but something is hampering their comm devices. Lazaro thinks it's some kind of a signal block."

Sia's heart sank with dread as each second ticked past. "Where is Trygg, Melena?"

"He's on the ship. He jumped on board by himself as it was leaving port." She shook her head in sober apology. "Lazaro doesn't know if any of his attempts to reach Trygg have gone through or not."

"Someone has to warn him." Panic flooded her, along with a crippling sense of grief.

No. Whatever this trap of Santino's might be, it would not claim Trygg. He was too strong for that. Too smart.

But that didn't keep the fear from taking hold of her.

The man she loved was in danger, cut off from communication and possibly totally unaware that he and his comrades had just played right into Santino's hands.

"Someone needs to find Trygg before it's too late."

Melena nodded. "Lazaro and Savage are working on that. They'll get him, Sia."

"What if they don't?" Her voice rose along with her alarm. "What if they're too late?"

Anxiously, she paced over to the large illuminated map on the war room wall. Two red dots glowed in the area of Naples. The third was missing. Trygg's signal, cut off by the same block preventing his teammates from reaching him.

"Where is the cargo ship located?"

"I don't know exactly," Melena said. "Lazaro didn't say."

"Find out, Melena. Do it quickly. Please."

"All right." She called her mate and asked him for the information.

When it seemed to take more than a few seconds for the reply, Sia marched over and took the phone out of her friend's hand.

"I need the exact coordinates, Lazaro. As close as you can pinpoint."

She stood in front of the map as he rattled off an approximate location several miles out to sea. Sia concentrated on that spot on the map. It wasn't exact, but it would have to do.

It might be the only hope she had.

Sia tossed the phone back to Melena, then turned all of her focus onto the bracelet on her wrist. The tiny orb of Atlantean crystal began to glow. It kept burning brighter, until it finally lit up like a supernova.

And then she was gone.

Chapter 14

Sia splashed down into cold, dark water.

Her body plunged below the surface, down and down and down, as giant waves rolled above her. A sudden, bright orange light erupted as she struggled to climb back up. The percussion shook the sea all around her, her head throbbing with the sudden boom of a massive explosion.

No!

She fought her way to the surface, gulping in mouthfuls of salt water with each panicked cry.

No. She couldn't be too late.

"Trygg!" She started screaming his name the instant her head emerged from the waves.

The sea lapped at her face, briny and cold. Filling her lungs, soaking her clothes, the waves threatened to drag her under. She swam toward the fireball that bobbed several hundred yards away, her heart breaking as she stared at the total obliteration of what had been the cargo ship Lazaro had directed her to.

"Trygg!"

Sia swiped at her salt-crusted eyes and peered into the darkness. But as she searched the waves and floating debris, he was nowhere to be found.

She sucked in a mouthful of air and dove down, forcing her eyes open and using her preternaturally keen sight to look for shapes in the black water.

The search was grueling, horrific. Trygg hadn't been the only man on board Santino's booby-trapped ship. Sia swam past limbs and other grotesque remnants of the crew who'd apparently been unaware they were sailing to their deaths.

But then she saw the large shape of a man she'd know anywhere.

And to her relief, Trygg's body was intact.

She swam to him, propelled by a grim sense of elation. He was alive. But he was unconscious in the water, his face down, bleeding profusely. By some miracle, he had survived the explosion, but it wouldn't take long for the sharks to come. There was no time to assess the severity of his wounds. She needed to get him on dry land first.

The lights of Naples and the rest of Italy's coastline twinkled in the far distance. Sia could make the long swim with Trygg in tow, but the steep, jagged island of Capri was closer.

She swam with Trygg's unmoving body into the arched shelter of a cave at the base of the rocky island, calling upon her Atlantean strength and speed to take them there swiftly. Laying him gently on the small, sandy incline inside, she tore away his shredded black clothing and took in the extent of his injuries.

She wanted to be thankful that he was alive, but his wounds were far more severe than she'd realized in the water. Everywhere she looked, his skin was torn and riddled with lacerations and contusions. His face too. His rugged, scarred, beautiful face.

"Oh, Trygg," she whispered, leaning down to rest her cheek against his. "I'm sorry I didn't reach you sooner. Please wake up."

He was Breed, and while she didn't know how long it had been since he'd last fed, no amount of human blood would be able to mend so many injuries. And these were just the ones she could see. Internally, he must be hurting too.

Before long, he would be dying.

Sia could do nothing to stifle the sob that broke loose from her throat. "Trygg, please don't leave me. I love you. I can't lose you like this."

He didn't respond. His breathing was shallow, too slow.

He needed blood badly.

If he had a Breedmate like Melena or Bella, their blood might be strong enough to nourish his dying cells and organs before death took him. But Trygg needed something even more powerful than that.

Sia had the power to save him.

Her Atlantean blood was immortal. She could revive him, but like a Breedmate, to feed him her blood meant binding him to her forever. But worse than that, she would be doing it without his consent.

Shackling him to her much the same way he had been enslaved by Dragos and then Vicky. Except that with Sia, that shackle would be unbreakable.

It would be forever.

She couldn't think of anything she'd enjoy more than having him at her side for the rest of her days, but Trygg might disagree. He might despise her for taking the choice away from him, even if death was the only other alternative.

He choked on blood and water, tiny bubbles spilling over his lips. She didn't have much time to decide. If she waited much longer, not even she could save him.

On a miserable groan, she pulled one of his daggers loose from its sheath on his belt. The blade glinted like quicksilver in the darkness of the grotto.

"Forgive me," she whispered, then sliced the edge of the razor-sharp steel into her wrist and held the bleeding wound to his mouth.

* * * *

Trygg's senses came back online as if he'd been jump-started by the sun itself.

Light poured into him, warm and silky and profoundly powerful. Wave upon wave roared through his body, mending every limb and organ, infusing every cell. Bringing him back from the depths of a cold blackness that he was certain should have been his death.

Had been, he realized, as his conscious mind began piecing everything together.

The cargo ship.

The decoy shipment of Red Dragon.

The payload of hidden explosives that blew up just as he was leaping off the deck of the boat to escape Santino's trap.

And now this.

The light.

The power.

"*Sia?*" He opened his eyes and blinked in the darkness of a dank stone cave.

She sat beside him on a small bed of sand, her knees bent, her face resting on her folded arms. She'd been weeping. Tears streaked her beautiful face as she lifted her head and looked over at him.

"Trygg." His name was a breathless whisper, filled with relief. And regret.

"Where are we?" His voice was groggy with misuse and the likely gallons of salt water he'd ingested after the detonation had thrown him into the sea for God knew how long.

And then he realized what Sia's presence beside him actually meant.

"You came after me?" It sounded like an accusation and she flinched. "Sia, what the fuck were you thinking?"

She shook her head. "Lazaro said he lost contact with you. Someone had to warn you that Santino's boat was a trap. Someone had to try to reach you in time—"

"Not you, damn it!" He choked on the words, his lungs still waterlogged and raw. "You're the last person I'd want to risk something as reckless as that."

"I was the only one who could," she replied. "The crystal took me to the boat's location, but I was too late. It exploded just as I got there."

He stared at this Atlantean female—this woman who was as brave as any warrior he'd ever known—and felt his chest swell with pride. And with gratitude.

A host of tender emotions swamped him, all of them centered on Sia.

He glanced at her folded hands and frowned. Her wrists were empty. "You lost your crystal."

She shrugged. "It fell off somewhere in the water when I was bringing you here."

"I'll help you find it," he offered lamely. "I'll see to it that you get another one. If that's what you want."

"That's not what I want, Trygg." Fresh tears spilled down her cheeks. She swiped at them, turning her face away from him.

He rose up, taking a moment to assess what had to be catastrophic injuries from the explosion and his crash into the sea. But he saw no marks on his body at all. He felt no aches from broken bones or bruises.

He'd never felt stronger or more powerful in his life.

And his face… Christ, even that felt different now. The familiar tug of his scar each time he moved his lips or blinked his eye was gone.

He reached up to feel for the jagged line, but it was no longer there. His face was healed.

It only took him an instant to understand why. "You gave me your blood."

"I'm sorry," she murmured. "I didn't know what else to do. You were injured so badly when I found you in the water and I—"

"Why did you do it?" A curse blasted out of him as the full realization of what she had done sank into his brain. He took her quivering chin on the tips of his fingers and drew her gaze back to his. "Why did you come after me, Sia?"

"Because I love you."

All his breath left him in an astonished gust. "You shouldn't. You should save your love for a man who's more deserving. Someone gentler. Someone cleaner. These hands are stained with blood, Sia. They always will be. They're not the kind of hands that should be touching you."

"I don't want anyone else. I choose you." She squared her shoulders, some of the haughty, regal Atlantean pushing past the selfless, tender woman he also knew her to be. "I've chosen, Trygg. There is only you."

He held her gaze, unable to resist the urge to smooth his fingers along the soft curve of her cheek. "That's why you fed me your blood?"

"I couldn't let you die, Trygg. Even if that meant you would live the rest of your life hating me for the gift."

He listened without speaking, considering what it was going to mean to be bound to her forever. No other woman would be able to quench his thirst. No other woman would inflame his desire the way his blood would now call for Sia. She was a part of him irrevocably.

He stepped in close to her, craving her warmth already…always. "For most of my life, I only knew how to hate the chains that bound me. Now you've placed a new one on me."

She closed her eyes, remorse filling her lovely face. "I know, Trygg. And I'm sorr—"

He silenced her with a deep, unhurried kiss. "I'm not sorry, Sia. I can't think of any greater gift than the one you've given me now. Your blood. Your bond. Your love."

A soft cry slipped past her lips. "I thought you would despise me."

"No, Tamisia. I love you."

He took her face between his palms and kissed her again, savoring the taste of her. Through the bond of her blood, he could feel the depth of her affection for him. Her love was a light that glowed inside her, filling his own heart with an unearthly, extraordinary warmth.

This was how it would be between them from now on, her vitality and emotion flowing inside him. Instead of holding him down, this shackle freed him.

It unleashed a staggering desire within him.

"Sia," he murmured, drawing her against him as their kiss ignited into something neither of them could contain. "You're mine now."

"Yes," she whispered against his lips. "Only yours, Trygg."

His fangs responded as swiftly as the rest of him. Sia licked her lips, seeming to understand what he needed. Her hungered expression told him that she needed the same thing.

He eased her down onto the soft sand with him. They peeled away the damp, tattered rags of their clothing, and then Trygg was inside her, both of them moving together in a tempo as worshipful as it was urgent. There was no cooling their desire, no slowing their shared, intense release.

"Drink from me," he murmured, the glow of his irises bathing her milky skin in warm amber light as he rocked inside her. With his eyes on hers, he bit into his own wrist, opening twin punctures in his veins. "I need to know you'll be mine forever, my beautiful Tamisia."

"Oh, Trygg," she murmured, a pleasured smile curving her lips in the instant before her tongue touched his skin. "I already am."

He tipped his head back on a groan of pure ecstasy as she closed her mouth over his wounds and began to take her fill.

Epilogue

Crisp salt air lashed at Trygg's face as the fishing boat cut through the dark waves. Seated alongside him on a bench at the stern of the old vessel, Sia huddled close beneath the warmth of a thick blanket, her arms wrapped around his torso.

As far as romance went, their moonlit ride back to the mainland left something to be desired. Lazaro had been on the satellite phone with Lucan for the past ten minutes, while Savage manned the helm.

"Santino's dead," the commander said as he ended the call to D.C.

"What?" Trygg leaned forward, torn between elation and a morbid disappointment that he hadn't been the one to personally send the bastard on his way to hell.

Lazaro nodded. "It just happened about an hour ago. Turns out one of the boys Santino abused held a grudge. Ten years later, the kid comes back all grown up and shoots the son of a bitch dead while he was asleep."

Savage threw a smirk over his shoulder. "Revenge really is a dish best served cold."

"Anyway," Lazaro said, "Santino is out of the way, but that doesn't mean someone else won't be stepping up to take his place. Red Dragon is too profitable, and too effective as a weapon against us, to expect anyone to let it lie untapped."

"Then we'll keep taking the assholes out until we root out every last bit of that poison," Sia said.

Trygg chuckled. "Careful. You're starting to sound like one of us."

She arched a brow at him. "Something wrong with that, warrior?"

He grinned. "No, ma'am. Not a thing."

"That's better." She took his face in her hands and kissed him hard, not seeming to care at all that his commander and one of his comrades were looking on.

To Trygg's amazement, he didn't care either.

After a moment, Lazaro cleared his throat. "I suppose this means you won't be asking me for any more letters of recommendation after all, Sia?"

She drew away from Trygg's mouth and smiled at Lazaro. "Not unless you'd like to write one to Lucan Thorne."

The commander smirked. "That could probably be arranged."

Trygg nipped her earlobe. "Don't you think we should talk about this first?"

"We just did. Partner."

He groaned, but there was no bite to it. "I can't think of anyone I'd rather have at my side, Sia. In the Order, and in life."

"That's good," she said. "Because that's exactly where I plan to stay. Forever."

He chuckled, pressing another kiss to her lips as he dragged the blanket over their heads, content to let his duty, his brothers-in-arms, and the rest of the world fade away for a while.

* * * *

Also from 1001 Dark Nights and Lara Adrian, discover MIDNIGHT UNTAMED, TEMPTED BY MIDNIGHT and STROKE OF MIDNIGHT.

Sign up for the 1001 Dark Nights Newsletter
and be entered to win a Tiffany Key necklace.

There's a contest every month!

Go to www.1001DarkNights.com to subscribe.

As a bonus, all subscribers will receive a free
1001 Dark Nights story
The First Night
by Lexi Blake & M.J. Rose

Discover 1001 Dark Nights Collection Four

Go to www.1001DarkNights.com for more information.

ROCK CHICK REAWAKENING by Kristen Ashley
A Rock Chick Novella

ADORING INK by Carrie Ann Ryan
A Montgomery Ink Novella

SWEET RIVALRY by K. Bromberg

SHADE'S LADY by Joanna Wylde
A Reapers MC Novella

RAZR by Larissa Ione
A Demonica Underworld Novella

ARRANGED by Lexi Blake
A Masters and Mercenaries Novella

TANGLED by Rebecca Zanetti
A Dark Protectors Novella

HOLD ME by J. Kenner
A Stark Ever After Novella

SOMEHOW, SOME WAY by Jennifer Probst
A Billionaire Builders Novella

TOO CLOSE TO CALL by Tessa Bailey
A Romancing the Clarksons Novella

HUNTED by Elisabeth Naughton
An Eternal Guardians Novella

EYES ON YOU by Laura Kaye
A Blasphemy Novella

BLADE by Alexandra Ivy/Laura Wright
A Bayou Heat Novella

DRAGON BURN by Donna Grant
A Dark Kings Novella

TRIPPED OUT by Lorelei James
A Blacktop Cowboys® Novella

STUD FINDER by Lauren Blakely

MIDNIGHT UNLEASHED by Lara Adrian
A Midnight Breed Novella

HALLOW BE THE HAUNT by Heather Graham
A Krewe of Hunters Novella

DIRTY FILTHY FIX by Laurelin Paige
A Fixed Novella

THE BED MATE by Kendall Ryan
A Room Mate Novella

PRINCE ROMAN by CD Reiss
A Games Novella

NO RESERVATIONS by Kristen Proby
A Fusion Novella

DAWN OF SURRENDER by Liliana Hart
A MacKenzie Family Novella

Discover 1001 Dark Nights Collection One

Discover 1001 Dark Nights Collection Two

Go to www.1001DarkNights.com for more information.

WICKED WOLF by Carrie Ann Ryan
WHEN IRISH EYES ARE HAUNTING by Heather Graham
EASY WITH YOU by Kristen Proby
MASTER OF FREEDOM by Cherise Sinclair
CARESS OF PLEASURE by Julie Kenner
ADORED by Lexi Blake
HADES by Larissa Ione
RAVAGED by Elisabeth Naughton
DREAM OF YOU by Jennifer L. Armentrout
STRIPPED DOWN by Lorelei James
RAGE/KILLIAN by Alexandra Ivy/Laura Wright
DRAGON KING by Donna Grant
PURE WICKED by Shayla Black
HARD AS STEEL by Laura Kaye
STROKE OF MIDNIGHT by Lara Adrian
ALL HALLOWS EVE by Heather Graham
KISS THE FLAME by Christopher Rice
DARING HER LOVE by Melissa Foster
TEASED by Rebecca Zanetti
THE PROMISE OF SURRENDER by Liliana Hart

Also from 1001 Dark Nights

THE SURRENDER GATE By Christopher Rice
SERVICING THE TARGET By Cherise Sinclair

Discover 1001 Dark Nights Collection Three

Go to www.1001DarkNights.com for more information.

About Lara Adrian

LARA ADRIAN is the *New York Times* and #1 internationally best-selling author of the Midnight Breed vampire romance series, with nearly 4 million books in print and digital worldwide and translations licensed to more than 20 countries. Her books regularly appear in the top spots of all the major bestseller lists including the *New York Times*, *USA Today*, *Publishers Weekly*, Indiebound, Amazon.com, Barnes & Noble, etc.

Lara Adrian's debut title, Kiss of Midnight, was named Borders Books best-selling debut romance of 2007. Later that year, her third title, Midnight Awakening, was named one of Amazon.com's Top Ten Romances of the Year. Reviewers have called Lara's books "addictively readable" (Chicago Tribune), "extraordinary" (Fresh Fiction), and "one of the best vampire series on the market" (Romantic Times).

With an ancestry stretching back to the Mayflower and the court of King Henry VIII, Lara Adrian lives with her husband in New England, surrounded by centuries-old graveyards, hip urban comforts, and the endless inspiration of the broody Atlantic Ocean.

Connect with Lara online:

Website: www.LaraAdrian.com

Discover More Lara Adrian

Midnight Untamed
A Midnight Breed Novella
By Lara Adrian

The mission was supposed to be simple. Infiltrate an enemy's stronghold outside Rome and eliminate its leader. For a Breed warrior as lethal as Ettore Selvaggio, AKA "Savage," stealth assassinations are only one of his many cold-hearted specialties. But the last thing Savage expects to find behind enemy lines—in his target's bed—is a woman he once adored.

It's been years since Savage last saw beautiful Arabella Genova. Years he's strived to banish to his past, along with the fierce desire he once felt toward Bella...and the irresistible calling of her blood that stirs in him even now, despite the fact that she belongs to another male.

But when fate throws Savage and Bella together again in a race for their lives, will his long-lost love prove to be the one woman he can't live without, or the perfect weapon to destroy him?

* * * *

Stroke of Midnight
A Midnight Breed Novella
By Lara Adrian

Born to a noble Breed lineage steeped in exotic ritual and familial duty, vampire warrior Jehan walked away from the luxurious trappings of his upbringing in Morocco to join the Order's command center in Rome.

But when a generations-old obligation calls Jehan home, the reluctant desert prince finds himself thrust into an unwanted handfasting with Seraphina, an unwilling beauty who's as determined as he is to resist the antiquated pact between their families.

Yet as intent as they are to prove their incompatibility, neither can deny the attraction that ignites between them. And as Jehan and

Seraphina fight to resist the calling of their blood, a deadly enemy seeks to end their uneasy truce before it even begins....

* * * *

Tempted By Midnight
A Midnight Breed Novella
By Lara Adrian

Once, they lived in secret alongside mankind. Now, emerged from the shadows, the Breed faces enemies on both sides—human and vampire alike. No one knows that better than Lazaro Archer, one of the eldest and most powerful of his kind. His beloved Breedmate and family massacred by a madman twenty years ago, Lazaro refuses to open his heart again.

Sworn to his duty as the leader of the Order's command center in Italy, the last thing the hardened warrior wants is to be tasked with the rescue and safekeeping of an innocent woman in need of his protection. But when a covert mission takes a deadly wrong turn, Lazaro finds himself in the unlikely role of hero with a familiar, intriguing beauty he should not desire, but cannot resist.

Melena Walsh has never forgotten the dashing Breed male who saved her life as a child. But the chivalrous hero of her past is in hard contrast to the embittered, dangerous man on whom her safety now depends. And with an unwanted—yet undeniable—desire igniting between them, Melena fears that Lazaro's protection may come at the price of her heart....

Midnight Unbound
A Midnight Breed Novella
By Lara Adrian

As a former Hunter bred to be a killing machine in the hell of a madman's lab, Breed vampire Scythe is a dangerous loner whose heart has been steeled by decades of torment and violence. He has no room in his world for love or desire--especially when it comes in the form of a vulnerable, yet courageous, Breedmate in need of protection. Scythe has loved--and lost--once before, and paid a hefty price for the weakness of his emotions. He's not about to put himself in those chains again, no matter how deeply he hungers for lovely Chiara.

For Chiara Genova, a widow and mother with a young Breed son, the last thing she needs is to put her fate and that of her child in the hands of a lethal male like Scythe. But when she's targeted by a hidden enemy, the obsidian-eyed assassin is her best hope for survival…even at the risk of her heart.

* * * *

It was long past midnight by the time Scythe pulled into the vineyard's twisting driveway at the base of Mount Vulture. After several hours behind the wheel, he was twitchy with the need for freedom. He'd elected to take Chiara's Fiat instead of his SUV in the hopes of avoiding notice on the road, a decision he'd regretted more and more with each passing mile. At six-foot-six, his head grazed the ceiling of the tiny vehicle and he had to spread his legs wide in order to accommodate the steering wheel between them.

He felt like a bear trapped in a chicken coop.

Even worse than the discomfort of his cramped muscles was the distraction of Chiara's close proximity in the tight quarters of the car. He could smell the citrusy freshness of her skin and hair, could feel the warmth of her body seated beside him. He could hear the shallow rhythm of her breathing as the silence stretched on between them, could almost feel the frantic beating of her heart like a vibration in his own veins.

She stirred other parts of him too. For a Hunter who'd been ruthlessly trained to deny his own wants and needs in favor of duty and self-control, his road trip with Chiara had been a startling reminder of the fact that beneath it all, he was still, ultimately, a flesh-and-blood male. A male who couldn't ignore the soft, beautiful female confined in the small space along with him, no matter how hard he tried.

Even now, his cock rested heavily between his thighs, a throbbing, heated reminder of just how long he'd gone without slaking that other hunger. Under his clothing, the Breed *dermaglyphs* that tracked all over his skin felt tingly and alive, no doubt infusing with all of the deep, changeable colors of his desire. He swallowed on an arid throat and his tongue grazed over the tips of his emerging fangs.

Damn, this wasn't good.

Although he wanted to blame his awareness of Chiara on simple, unchecked lust, the truth was he couldn't recall the last time his body had challenged his iron-hewn will.

Then again, yes he could.

It was only six weeks ago. Back in Matera, when he'd first laid eyes on Chiara Genova.

"Fuck."

She glanced at him, frowning. He didn't have to wonder if she saw the flecks of amber glowing in the blackness of his irises. Her swift intake of breath told him so.

Hopefully she'd assume the sparks were due to irritation, rather than desire. Both emotions were riding him in equal measure, after all.

"Something wrong, Scythe?"

"Yeah. If this winds up taking longer than a couple of days, we're going to need to talk about another mode of transportation."

"You're the one who suggested we take my car," she reminded him.

There was a note to her voice he hadn't heard before and he swiveled a questioning look at her. In the thin light of the dashboard, he saw that her lips were twitching. With a start, he realized that she was struggling not to laugh at him. He had only thought about how uncomfortable it was, but he had to imagine he looked as ridiculous as he felt.

He scowled at her, but his heart wasn't in it.

"I'm sorry," she said, a giggle slipping past her lips. "I really shouldn't laugh. It's just... I'm sorry, it's really not funny. It's just that you're so big and this car is so small. You look like you're driving a dollhouse car. I don't know how you've managed to make this whole trip without getting a nasty Charlie horse in your thigh."

Jesus Christ.

Didn't she realize? A Charlie horse was the least of his discomforts.

He stared at her as she struggled to keep the humor out of her expression. Tried and failed, that is. Another laugh burst out of her. She waved her hand in front of her face as if in apology, but it was no use. Her laughter filled the car, and as prickly and on edge as he felt, he took a strange comfort in the sound.

It was as if a valve had been opened and all of the weight of what had happened—the grim reality of why they both were seated in this vehicle together in the first place—released with each soft giggle that rolled off Chiara's tongue.

"Are you finished?" he asked, feeling less impatient than his gruff voice suggested.

Deep down, though, he was relieved. Hearing about her harrowing ordeal had him on the razor's edge, too, and filled with a fury that he couldn't justify, but couldn't deny. Her distress at leaving Pietro was almost palpable, and if his discomfort behind the wheel of her miniature vehicle made her forget about all of that for even an instant, he should be thankful.

Having her at ease would make his job all the simpler. She would be more amenable to his instructions, more trusting of him. Less likely to question or challenge his commands when her life depended on letting him handle the lethal business he was born and bred to do.

He doused the headlights as he drove the car up the drive, parking beside the villa and killing the engine. "Stay here. I need to check the perimeter of the house and inside. Once it's clear, I'll come back for you."

She shook her head and started to open her mouth, but he held up his hand to silence her.

"You will follow my orders without questions or argument. That was our agreement, remember?"

"I wasn't going to argue," she replied stiffly, the grin that had been tugging at her lips just a moment before fading away like the sun at dusk. "I was just going to tell you that I had an alarm system installed in the villa a few weeks ago. In order to disarm it, you have to enter the code. Five, seven, seven, eight."

Right.

He handed her the car keys, making sure not to touch her when he did. If he made physical contact with her after the torturous drive, or while the sweet scent of her still clung to his senses and the bright sound of her laughter was still echoing in his ears, he was liable to lose his mind.

Or worse, give in to the hunger she awakened in him.

Alone in his dark den of solitude, it was easier to ignore the pull of the flesh. Here with a beautiful, unmated female so close, he was playing with fire. And Chiara Genova made him want to burn.

Not good at all.

"Slide over to the driver's side and lock the door when I leave," he commanded in a brusque voice. "If I'm not back in five minutes, don't come inside. Start the car and drive away as fast as you can. Head straight back to the Order headquarters. Understand?"

"Scythe, if you think I would turn around and leave you here by your—"

"Damn it, woman." His frustration exploded out of him, motivated chiefly by concern for her. "Just tell me you'll fucking do what I say."

She drew back, her cheeks going pale at his sharp rebuke. "All right, Scythe. I will. I'll stay until you come for me."

There was a spark of indignation, even defiance, in her wide brown eyes, but he didn't have time to test her. Nor did he have the time—or the skills—to try to soothe her. He had a job to do, and the less he had to worry about ruffling her feathers or calming her afterward, the better things would be for both of them.

Regardless of that, he dug deep and called up an image of young Pietro to remind himself of exactly what was at stake here for both of them. Of course, things were tense. It was a life or death situation and she was now separated from her child for the first time. Even Scythe had to admit she was handling it better than he'd expected.

"Five minutes, Chiara. If I don't return by then, leave and don't look back."

He exited the car, sniffing the night air for signs of trouble. So far, his danger antenna was still, and he didn't detect anything out of the ordinary. Fertile, rich soil, the sharp scent of fermentation, sugary grapes and the luscious sweetness of Chiara's skin permeated his senses and he blocked it out with a muttered oath.

He moved stealthily around the back of the sprawling villa to the door that opened into the kitchen. The locks turned free under the power of his mind, then he opened the door and entered on silent feet. No need for Chiara's alarm code; he disabled the flashing sensors with a flick of his thoughts as he stepped farther inside the darkened house.

No signs of trouble as he gazed around the kitchen and into the great room. The place was quiet, no one here now and no evidence that anyone had been there in the time since Chiara had left earlier tonight. The sense of malevolence Scythe would have felt if there was a threat of imminent danger inside the villa was notably absent.

Although he trusted his innate ability, he still made a quick sweep of every room and every point of entry. When it came to keeping Chiara safe, he was leaving nothing left to chance.

Each second she was unprotected and out of his sight as he searched the house felt like an hour. He couldn't deny the relief that washed over him when he returned to the car where she waited and found her sitting there, just as he'd instructed, safe and sound behind the wheel.

"All clear," he murmured, as he opened the driver's side door and helped her out.

She met his gaze with a disgruntled glance, then followed him back to the villa in chilly silence. When she reached for the light switch near the kitchen door, Scythe caught her hand and stilled it.

"No lights for now. It's the middle of the night, and we don't want this place lit up like a beacon if anyone's watching. It was risk enough driving up here together at this late hour."

She nodded, slowly withdrawing her fingers from his loose grasp. The warmth of her skin lingered against his palm, sending heat licking up his arm, through his veins...into the distracting thickness at his groin.

"Go on," he commanded her curtly. "Get settled and try to rest. I'll handle things on my end. I need to get the tactical equipment from the car, and I plan to set up some surveillance points around the property before sunrise."

She nodded, but remained standing in front of him. Too damned close for his peace of mind. "There's a small guest room down the hall from the master bedroom. I didn't know to prepare it for you ahead of time, but it'll only take me a few minutes to—"

"No." His sharp reply cut her off. "I won't be sleeping more than a few minutes at a time while I'm on this assignment, and I sure as hell don't plan to get comfortable in a bed."

Least of all in one just steps away from hers.

"Fine." Her lips pressed flat as she stared up at him. "I was only trying to help."

"Don't bother," he snapped. "I can take care of myself. I've been doing it for a long time."

Finally, she retreated, moving back a step. He almost breathed a sigh of relief that she was going—but then instead of pivoting away, she crossed her arms over her breasts and advanced on him, pinning him with a glare.

"Is this how you treat everyone who tries to show you a little kindness? I know I agreed to do what you asked while you're here, but do you plan to scowl and bark orders at me the whole time?"

He scrubbed his hand over his face in frustration. What had happened to the Chiara he'd met six weeks ago in Matera? While he wouldn't have described her as meek, he hadn't seen this kind of fire in her then. That Chiara had seemed so vulnerable. Fragile with fear and uncertainty.

Sure, he had admired her obvious devotion to her son, and he'd seen the kindness that radiated from her. He had appreciated her beauty more than he had a right to—that part of her had been impossible to ignore or to forget in all the time since. How many times had he been tempted to venture out to Potenza just for another glimpse of her? How many times had he woken from fevered dreams where he had Chiara naked in his arms, moaning in pleasure?

Christ, too many to count. But he'd resisted, knowing a delicate female like Chiara would crumble in his ungentle hands like a dried rose petal.

This woman before him, her warm brown eyes flashing, pert breasts heaving with her indignation, was someone else entirely. And damned if he didn't want this new Chiara even more.

He'd been brought in to protect her, yet all he could think about right now was how sweet she must taste. Not what he'd come here to do.

She took his silence as an opportunity to press further.

"I don't know why you agreed to watch over me when it's obvious you'd rather be doing anything else. But like it or not, it appears we're stuck with each other for the time being."

"Yes, we are," he agreed. "So, do us both a favor and try to pretend I'm not here."

She balked. "You can't be serious. When's the last time you looked in a mirror? You're not exactly easy to miss."

Neither was she, and he'd realized the idiocy of his suggestion as soon as he said it. Still, he hoped his gruffness would push her away, if only for his peace of mind. He had numerous things to do yet tonight and arguing with Chiara wasn't going to get any of them done.

All it was doing was making him twitchy with the need to silence her, even if he had to do it with his own mouth on hers.

"I'm not going to walk around on eggshells in my own home, Scythe. And no matter what you say, I'm not going to forget for a second why you're here. My life is in your hands. Do you think that means nothing to me?" She expelled a short laugh. "While we're on the subject, did you actually think I would've driven off and left you here to die alone if there had been trouble when we arrived?"

Yes, he had. He'd more than thought it, he'd expected her to follow his instructions to the letter. "I wouldn't have died, Chiara. I've gone up against a dozen Breed males at a time and walked away the only one still breathing. Your stalker won't be any match for me. Killing is what I was born to do."

It took her a moment to absorb that. "Well, either way, I wouldn't have left. What kind of person do you imagine I am?"

He knew she didn't expect him to answer, so he didn't voice any of the replies that popped into his mind.

A foolish one.

A stubborn one.

A beautiful one.

A brave one.

"I may not have asked you to play my protector, Scythe, but I am grateful to have you."

She edged closer, leaving him no option but to hold his ground or back away from her advance. He chose the former, even though every instinct in his body warned him it was a mistake to let her any nearer.

"And I'm grateful for how you sheltered Pietro and me along with Bella and Ettore when we came to you in Matera too. Maybe none of that means anything to you, but it does to me. So you'll just have to forgive me for trying to be nice or hospitable to you."

A tendon pulsed in his jaw as he stared down at her. This was dangerous territory, allowing her to think of him as some sort of savior. Dangerous for him, and for her.

Rather than succumb to the urge to touch her, his left hand flexed and fisted at his side, while the stump on his right wrist throbbed in useless stillness.

It wasn't hard to recall the mistake that had cost him his other hand. He'd let his guard down once, had let emotion cloud his reason and paid a steep price for it. Not only him, but two other people he cared for.

Never again.

That lesson—that awful regret—would stay with him forever.

On behalf of 1001 Dark Nights,

Liz Berry and M.J. Rose would like to thank ~

Steve Berry
Doug Scofield
Kim Guidroz
Jillian Stein
InkSlinger PR
Dan Slater
Asha Hossain
Chris Graham
Fedora Chen
Kasi Alexander
Jessica Johns
Dylan Stockton
Richard Blake
BookTrib After Dark
and Simon Lipskar

72007346R00078

Made in the USA
San Bernardino, CA
22 March 2018